THE SWITCHBLADE SVENGALI

THE SWITCHBLADE SVENGALI

BY COY HALL

OTHER WORKS
BY COY HALL

A Séance for Wicked King Death

Grimoire of the Four Impostors

The Hangman Feeds the Jackal

A Pantheon of Thieves

The Promise of Plague Wolves

THE SWITCHBLADE SVENGALI

by Coy Hall

Published by **Shotgun Honey Books**

215 Loma Road
Charleston, WV 25314
www.ShotgunHoney.com

Cover Design by Ron Earl Phillips.

First Printing 2024.

ISBN-10: 1-956957-76-6
ISBN-13: 978-1-956957-76-1

9 8 7 6 5 4 3 2 1   24 23 22 21 20 19

For Olivia

THE
SWITCHBLADE
SVENGALI

The vamp drained me, but I couldn't withdraw from the conversation. Dame Theda Eklund, smashed on pills and champagne, reclined on a velvet cushion with her legs crossed. Her heels were off, tucked beneath the settee. A short, black wig covered her white hair, granting a touch of youth and radiance. Age didn't rob her of the sculpted jawline, perfect nose, and starlet eyes.

Presently, I returned with two flutes of vintage Dom Perignon. Bubbles danced behind the pearled glass in my hands. The Duprey sisters, our hosts, didn't serve cheap sparkling wine—the thought of such a thing mortified them—so they were my kind of people. Even with the tiresome talk, I was content, at home in my surroundings.

Theda regarded me with a drunken smile, accepting the flute. She lounged with a Marlboro in her hand, burning close to her long nails. There was a time when I imagined she would use a cigarette holder (she possessed that level of class in her silent films), but she was distant from the characters she portrayed on screen. For as long as I'd known her, she'd preferred Marlboro kings to fine tobacco. She smoked with the grace of a teamster, chewing on the filter, exhaling through her nose, spilling ash. Theda was an effortlessly foul woman.

"Dear, where in the hell were we?" she asked. The voice was gravelly. When high, her Brooklyn accent thickened.

I sat down beside her, my tuxedo broiling under the collar. Despite the cool desert air outside, the apartment was stuffy. The Dupreys never opened windows in fear that their dogs would rush onto the ledge, chasing birds. It was absurd. The dogs never even barked at birds.

I scanned the crowd for Dominic, hoping to find him bored and in want of attention, but he was animated, discussing something (probably the war) with two elderly gentlemen. He was fine, but his rambling perplexed the old men. Ten people milling about stood between us, so my pleading expression missed him. I wanted to step outside, to let some steam out of my waistcoat, but the vamp had me in her talons, and Dominic wasn't going to rescue me.

"Tod Browning, the director," I said. I leaned back, trying to relax. "You were in one of his pictures."

Theda sipped champagne. She smiled at the memory.

It wasn't that I didn't enjoy her stories, but I'd heard them, all of them, countless times. Theda only had so many tales to tell, and when she cornered me, she told them. Once, I had urged her to write a memoir, to exorcise the stories, but she said her escapades weren't interesting enough to warrant a book. That was true except for the one where she fucked John Barrymore and John Gilbert on the same night. That was a good one. Everybody needed to read that story.

"What an absolutely bizarre man Tod was, especially after his motorcar crash," she said. "Dear, the man was capable of great cruelty. He dovetailed so perfectly with Lon Chaney. They were quite the pair."

"It shows in his pictures," I said. "The penchant for cruelty."

"Does it? It's been so long."

"They're shown on television now," I said.

"I don't believe it."

"Oh, come on. I know you watch yourself."

Theda flicked ash, smirking. She didn't deny it.

"Tell me about making it with John Gilbert."

Theda snickered. "You're always so naughty, Royce," she said. She exhaled a cloud of smoke.

I smiled, and then I took a long drink of the Dom Perignon. It was too light to do the job of getting me drunk. "I like John Gilbert."

"Beautiful man, dear, but he hung four hard." Theda cackled.

"Oh, stop. No. You never said that before. You're just trying to ruin my fantasy. Do you ever regret not getting your claws into Rudy Valentino?" I asked.

"Lord, no. Rudolph was a bore. Speaking of bores, darling—"

Adelaide Duprey sauntered over, interrupting the conversation. Adelaide had boundless verve and energy, mingling with her guests like a persistent butterfly from the beginning of a party to the end. Florinda, the sister with whom she shared a home, was the opposite. She held court on a stool by the bar, receiving folks as they came to chat, rarely moving her bulk. Adelaide was pristine and flushed in a sequined dress of green, and properly silly with a hairpiece that stood on her head like antennae, spelling *Adieu 1967*. Florinda, at the beginning of the night, had the other half: her headpiece read *Hello 1968*.

Adelaide's Great Pyrenees, an enormous, human-sized white dog, walked at her side. At 150 pounds, the canine was larger than his master and an equal in stage presence. His name, Thibodeaux, was emblazoned on the American Kennel Club medallion attached to his collar. The animal was panting and hot, stressed by the crowd. He sat on his haunches. I'd kept Thibodeaux for a weekend once, so he and I were pals.

"Two of my favorite people," Adelaide said. She was drunk. She looked at the dog. "Say *bonjour*, Thibodeaux."

Dutifully, the dog raised his manicured paw.

Adelaide laughed from the belly. A widow who never had children, the dog was Adelaide's life. Her sister, Florinda, had a Pyrenees, too, the sibling of Thibodeaux. Her name was Drucilla, but she was too shy to mingle. Curiously, each dog mirrored the owner.

Thibodeaux knew three tricks, and this was the one we saw the most. Everyone at the party saw it at least once. The dog was more tired than amused, though. I knew the feeling. I winked at him. He panted at me, his plume of a tail wagged, and his eyes smiled.

"That's a good boy," I said, scratching his elegant snout.

Adelaide hovered over the sofa, humming along with a tacky Kay Kyser record that played on the hi-fi. *No one's taste is flawless. Case in point.* Her makeup was chic against pale skin, and her wig was marvelously natural, dark and straight, curling under at her neck—the Jackie Onassis model.

"You look a decade younger than last year," I told her.

Adelaide blushed.

"It's true, Addy. You don't look a day over forty-five. No thirty-five." I smiled.

Theda rolled her eyes.

"Don't be catty," Adelaide told her. "Royce knows beauty when he sees it. Don't you, dear?"

"Well, I don't feel any younger than seventy," Theda said. "Where'd you get that wig?"

"At Clayton's, dear, the same as you."

"I thought perhaps it came from Thib's groomer." Theda grinned at the dog.

Adelaide made a sour face, but this was love language. The two were the same in age and nearly as close as Adelaide and her sister. The three formed something of a family. They looked upon me as an adopted son and Dominic as a son-in-law.

I finished the champagne.

Adelaide pointed a jeweled finger at me. "I have you booked for next week," she said. "We'll do a proper séance to begin the year. I'll have a woman over who lost her son in Cambodia. He was a photojournalist. I think you should give her proper attention, dear. She's quite desperate for comfort."

I nodded solemnly. "I'll do what I can," I said.

"But *tonight,* I want you to do a little something for *me.*"

"She's superb at begging favors," Theda said. "She has an endless capacity for it." Theda drained the rest of her champagne and handed me the glass.

"You can't act like a child at seventy," Adelaide said. "How do you manage to do it, dear?"

"Oh, that's where you're going." Theda turned to me. "I heard her say *groovy* last week. I swear to Osiris, she said it on Christmas Eve. Ask Florinda. We were aghast."

"It was an effort to be humorous. A failed one."

"You can't be funny and seventy, either. Not intentionally."

"Go ahead, Addy," I said, smiling at Theda. Awkwardly, with the side table full of ashtrays, I rotated the empty flutes in my hands. The dog licked one. I let him. "What would you like?" Performing was the last thing I wanted to do, but I owed her favors—more than I could repay. Inside, my stomach turned at the thought. Outwardly, I was genial.

Adelaide scratched her dog's ears. Thib closed his eyes with pleasure. He stopped licking the glass.

"I was telling a couple who know of you but don't *know* you that you're in the business of hypnotism now. Of course, that intrigued them, but they scarce believe in hypnotists. They joked about *Svengali*. Is it too much to ask, Royce, for you to speak to them? You don't have to perform, dear."

"Skeptics," Theda said. The vamp sensed my displeasure, so she fed. She edged closer until her perfume enveloped me. The fragrance was more expensive than the champagne.

I grimaced.

"Oh, please, dear. It means so much to me. You know how it rattles me to hear your talents questioned. It positively enrages me." Adelaide frowned with gravity.

"Why not show them the door?" Theda asked.

"I just might. After."

"What would you do if they said you're a fraud?" Theda asked me. "A charlatan? Directly to your face."

"If they called me a charlatan, I'd ask what century they were from."

"Funny guy."

If you only knew, I thought.

"The world's full of skeptics," I said. "It wouldn't be the first time someone said it to my face."

"Please, Royce dear?"

"Of course I will."

Adelaide clapped her hands. "Come, come," she said.

I handed the glasses to Theda and stood.

"Knock 'em dead, Svengali," she said. She threw back her head and laughed.

Reluctantly, I followed Adelaide and Thibodeaux to the bar. It was a fine slab backed by crystal and mirrors. As we wedged through the crowd, people ignored me and patted the dog.

The Duprey penthouse was modern, having undergone a redesign the decade prior. Several walls were knocked out to accommodate the look. There was a sunken living room, quite chic, and separate spaces for a kitchen and three bedrooms, but mostly it was an open concept. Florinda was quite the addict when it came to Italian movies, so she'd modeled the idea on what she knew from television. The penthouse occupied the entire top floor of a downtown high rise. The view outside was a garden of concrete and brick, a view nobody desired anymore. Most of the wealthy in town inhabited the suburbs, but not the Dupreys.

"Stay here," Adelaide said. "I'll gather them." She and the dog mixed into the crowd.

I walked to the bar and hugged Florinda around the shoulder. She sat alone, eating a plate of prosciutto-wrapped dates. Her *Hello 1968* headpiece lay on the rosewood counter, so I grabbed it and placed it on my head. She smiled, but she was morose.

"You seem to be enjoying yourself," Florinda said.

She didn't have the quaint good looks of her sister, or her butterfly manner, and she'd grown quite heavy since her husband had passed. She was two years older than Addy, but one would insist ten years separated them. I worried about her health more than she worried about it. She was, although she'd never admit it, locked in depression. Her condition had become existential. She depended on my private sessions for comfort. I did the best I could for her, communicating with her husband whenever she wished it.

"No, no, I'm not," I said. "Not at all. What are you drinking?" I lifted her glass and smelled. The liquor had the aroma of juniper. She was drunk on gin, which made me envious. I looked around for Adelaide. "Pour one for me, please," I said.

Florinda stood from the stool. She walked to the other side of the counter and lifted a crystal decanter that had been tucked away, hidden. She didn't stint. She poured me four fingers worth. There were no mixers in sight, but I liked gin straight. I took a drink.

"Grateful," I said. "Champagne is like candy to me."

"Is Addy bothering you?" Florinda asked. She reseated herself.

I shrugged.

"Do I need to tell her to stop?"

She offered the plate of dates. The tang of goat cheese, spread beneath the prosciutto, reached me. I declined.

"I owe her," I said, "but perhaps you should tell her to stop, regardless. Let's wait and see. Where's your dog?"

Florinda gestured at a closed door. "Hiding in the bedroom." She chuckled. "She can only fit her head under the bed, but she buries it like an ostrich, her fat bottom sticking out."

"Poor baby."

"She isn't the attention whore that Thib is. Or that person who Thib owns. Speak of the Devil." Florinda peered over her shoulder, then turned her back again, watching through the mirror.

I put my drink on the bar and wiped my hands clean.

Adelaide returned with two guests.

"Royce, this is Karl and Shea Landrum. Recently betrothed, I might add."

"Many congratulations," I said. "How do you do?"

"Karl, Shea, this is Royce Madigan. You, of course, met my sister, Florinda."

"I don't do tricks," Florinda said to the glass.

"Jolly fellow that she is," Adelaide said.

Karl shook my hand. In my business a cold read is vital, so I begin to form pictures of everyone the moment I meet them. Sometimes I'm right, sometimes wrong, but I can intuit a lot in the first few seconds. Karl Landrum had a look I saw often in Arizona. His hands and face were too tanned, his features shopworn but handsome. He was an expatriate from Los Angeles. It was in his bearing. He was "retired" like everybody who migrated here from LA. Nobody was certain from where these people derived income, except that they "owned property." When I heard that phrase, I assumed organized crime, but I'm dramatic.

Mrs. Landrum was three decades his junior. That told me more. She was demure and elfish, pretty with a modern short haircut jagged at the bangs. Her eyes were intelligent rather than daft. She had strong opinions, but you had to know her a few years to excavate them. I wondered if Karl heard them. I doubted it. She mirrored her husband because she was smart enough to mirror him. He had the money. I shook her hand, as well. It was manicured, elegant, soft. She'd stepped up from the middle class.

Florinda spun around and nodded her greeting. Karl didn't like her. When he looked at me, I sensed he didn't like anybody very much, including our host.

Journalist, I thought, changing my mind, drawing my conclusion. *That's it. A journalist. And a prick with bad intentions.*

"What can I do for you?" I asked.

"Frankly, I think hypnotism is bunk," Karl began. "I was telling our hostess as much. Bunkum and balderdash."

"Mr. Landrum," Adelaide said, shocked, "you weren't saying that at all. Not in that manner."

Karl smiled at her. She'd taken his bait. "I'm told that's your trade. You can put your ghosts and séances under that label, too." He had a rapid manner, Flash Casey style.

Journalist with a trust fund, I thought. I had no doubt.

"I saw it on an episode of *Dragnet*," he added. "Bunk. That's what Joe Friday calls it, so that's what I call it. Bunk."

"Flapdoodle?" I asked.

"Precisely."

"Tommyrot?"

"What's your point, sir?"

"Just admiring your vocabulary." I took another drink of gin, and I hated him. "You seem like a man who admires a clean-cut square like Joe Friday," I said.

"I'll throw him out the window if you like," Florinda whispered. She ate one of the dates like an empress on a litter.

I told her to hold that thought. I didn't rule it out.

"Mr. Landrum," I said, "I'll respectfully disagree with you. Now, if you'd like a demonstration, you'll have to pay for the pleasure. I won't stoop to parlor games."

"*Stoop* is a fine word," Karl said.

"It's a long way down to the front stoop and pavement," Florinda continued, louder now.

"We'll have a séance one week from tonight," Adelaide said, trying to save the situation. "Would you like an invitation? You'll be my guests."

I frowned at her.

"Bunk," Karl repeated.

I took another drink of gin. "Get bent," I said.

"I beg your pardon, sir?"

"Hmm? Oh, I said it'd be money well spent." I winked at his wife. "The séance, I mean."

"Sir—"

Surprisingly, Shea interrupted Karl. "Mr. Royce," she started, and her tone was oil and water in contrast to that of her husband. "Your last name is Madigan?"

The prying put me on guard. I had a past, a long one, and I didn't like thinking about it, let alone having other people think about it. I certainly didn't like the idea of the Duprey sisters thinking about it. Or the Landrums.

"That's right," I said. I forced a smile. A pinpoint of sweat emerged at my hairline.

"You see, Karl writes for the *Scientific American*. Otherwise, he's retired, but he does a column for skeptics."

"I employ the term *bunk* quite often in that series, sir."

"That's obvious," I said.

"There is a woman about town," Shea continued, "and she's inquiring about a Royce Pembrook." She pronounced the last name carefully. I withered at the sound of it. The name was such a weight, such a burden. "Pembrook. Not Madigan. The man she described, however, fits you perfectly. Are you also known as Pembrook?"

"And who is this woman?" I asked.

A chill passed through me despite the closeness and heat. I withstood the rush of memories and trauma. I knew who was asking about me. I knew who would travel so far to shine a light on me and watch me squirm.

"Why is that important?" Shea asked. There was a gleam in her eyes. She was smoother than Karl, but her intentions were the same. She fit with him better than I thought. Her charisma was the sincerity of her look. She disarmed.

"One likes to know the hunter when they're quarry," I said,

trying to be witty, trying to be carefree, failing at both. I was playing a character then, many miles from genuine. What an odious task that is when the universe turns its hateful eye on you. The champagne had me nauseous.

"Would you like to know what she said about you?"

I drank the gin. The alcohol was dizzying, and the stuffiness of the room closed in on me. I fought the change in demeanor, but I was faint.

"I couldn't imagine caring less about what this woman had to say."

Karl smiled.

"Well, no matter then. Her name is Anna Vogel. Should we put her in touch with you?"

I shook my head. "I'd rather not associate with a crank from the streets."

"Oh, we never said she was from the streets. How interesting that you inferred that." She looked at her husband. "Perhaps, he is psychic. She seemed to know you very well, too. She knew of your séances. She was in the same line, once."

"Bunk," Karl added.

"You'll excuse me," I said. "Pleasure to make your acquaintance. Happy New Year."

"Our pleasure entirely," Shea said. "Happy New Year. Oh," she added, "is your name Pembrook or isn't it?" She didn't wait for an answer. She knew one wasn't coming. Shea turned to Adelaide instead. "What a beautiful dog," she commented.

Adelaide shook her head. "How could you—" she began. I didn't hear the rest. The voices, the music, the rush of thoughts consumed what remained.

Florinda stood from the stool and walked with me. We moved to a window that overlooked downtown traffic.

Automobiles filled the street—red lights one way, yellow lights the other. Light filled the building across the way, all the windows aglow. It was bursting at the seams with light, bright as the sun. Despite the cold, crowds of pedestrians covered the sidewalk. Midnight neared. I no longer shared the excitement for a new year. I wanted the old one to continue.

Florinda put her hand on my back. She didn't say anything.

"Please find Dom," I said. "I want to leave."

She nodded, and her face showed anger. "Why would Addy do such a thing?"

"She didn't know," I said. She didn't, after all. I had to defend her. "They tricked her."

"My sister isn't an easy woman to trick."

I didn't say anything about that. "Please don't give her a hard time," I said.

Florinda moved into the crowd to find Dominic.

Anna Vogel, I thought, and I was sick. I thought Anna would die in prison, that she'd rot away like her husband. I'd believed that part of my life was dead forever. Of all people, though, I should know the past doesn't die.

I was scared and angry, and I wanted Dominic near. I wanted to be in the comfort and quiet of our home, not here, not in a strange place with the lights and the dark windows and so much noise up from the street. I had to think. In my reflection in the black glass, I saw the *Hello 1968* headpiece that jostled between my ears. I pulled it off, feeling foolish. I looked over my shoulder.

Florinda pulled Dom from yet another conversation. His eyes found me.

CHAPTER TWO

"Happy New Year, gentlemen," the doorman said.

He was a kid in uniform, sitting in a plush chair between two large ferns by the entrance. Fluorescent light flooded the carpeted, cozy lobby. Raucous noise from the street made his plight miserable, so he looked the part. To cover the festivities, a radio on the front desk played a Top Forty station with a New Year's Eve countdown. The DJ introduced Buffalo Springfield. An enormous clock on the wall said that midnight was only fifteen minutes distant. The kid stood, offered a smile, and then opened the door to allow our exit. Cool air rushed in.

"Happy New Year," Dominic said. "I hope you're not here the rest of the night."

Unlike me, Dom was chipper. He thought alcohol had upset my stomach, so he held my waist like he was escorting someone ill. I walked upright. I didn't need help. I wasn't drunk.

The doorman smiled, checking his watch. "Another hour."

"Good to hear," Dominic said. "Enjoy."

"You, as well, sir."

When we were on the street, I faced Dom. The crowd

noise covered any talking we might do. The cold air relaxed me, chasing away the claustrophobia.

"Tell me," Dominic coaxed.

He kept his hand on my waist. For pulling him from the party, embarrassing him, he wasn't perturbed. Rather, he watched me with concern. He loved me as much as I loved him.

"I want to go home," I said, and felt childish for it. I tried to pull myself together.

Dom frowned. He'd never liked fragile things. "Let's walk around the block," he offered. "Tell me what happened."

This was a decent part of town, and there were crowds, traffic, and police about. The chances of getting mugged were slim, although Dom had been mugged a few streets north of here a year prior. He wasn't bothered by that fact, and I wasn't, so we walked.

I looked up at the building in which the Duprey sisters lived. The windows in the top floor were alight all the way around. The sight represented much of my life. I had other clients, but the Dupreys sustained me. They ensured that Dominic and I lived well. The Landrums and Anna—they'd try to dismantle that.

Fuck me, I thought.

As far as I knew, Florinda had yet to defenestrate Karl and his wife. I hoped we'd be on the correct side of the building if that occurred.

Dom, shoving his hands in the pockets of his tuxedo, waited until I was ready to talk. His face was flush, his manner drunken.

We moved through a bulk of people, wading against the current. Everybody was happy, intoxicated, and distracted. Being invisible eased my deeper feelings of being exposed.

I lit a cigarette to quiet my anger. Letting the Chesterfield get into my lungs, I stopped beneath a streetlamp and observed the lighter. It was a Christmas gift from Genevieve Blum, one of my clients in the fifties. I still received Christmas and birthday cards from the Blums. They still gushed about how I spoke to their son, and Genevieve still believed I was the Count of Saint Germain. The seven-leaved saptaparna, sacred to theosophists, stamped the silver. The lighter, Genevieve Blum, and Anna Vogel had the same roots.

I looked up at Dominic. He still greased back his hair like he did in those days, although a pair of glasses gave the look more sophistication. He'd lost the leather jacket and rolled-up jeans. He was beautiful, although the ubiquitous tan in this part of the world had replaced his dewy complexion of old. He'd been so thin and pale once. Age didn't hurt him, though. Age added qualities. He'd done much to erase his hick origins in West Virginia—he'd transformed as I'd transformed, changed his name when I changed my name—but something of that time remained in him like it remained in me. When I carried so much of those days, it was silly to think I could outrun them.

"She asked if my name was Pembrook," I said finally.

Dominic took my lighter and lit a clove cigarette. He watched my eyes, trying to gauge why such a thing bothered me so.

"Changing your name isn't a crime, Royce." He exhaled from the corner of his mouth. "We haven't done much to hide your background." He was bothered, but he acted like he wasn't. "What else did she say? And who the hell are we talking about?"

I told him about Karl and Shea Landrum.

"They sound like shitbirds," he said. He took a drag,

loosened his collar. "That's not heavy enough to bother you. What happened?"

Saying it aloud made it real. I hesitated.

Dominic took my hand. That was one thing that had changed since we first met in 1956. It would have been dangerous to hold my hand like that in Huntington, where we'd met.

"Anna's out of prison," I said.

That landed. He sobered. "They told you that?"

I tossed the remainder of my Chesterfield to the concrete, pissing off a man in bell-bottoms. The ashes touched his shoe. He gave me a look, but I didn't engage him.

"Shea Landrum told me that. She took delight in telling it, too. She knows something, Dom."

"It's been over a decade. She can't—"

"Dom, Anna's in town." I tried to keep my voice down, to stay calm, but I was animated, my anger spilling. I wasn't invisible anymore. "Tonight, Dom. Anna's here. She talked to the Landrums. And the Landrums know me. They know the Dupreys." I gestured around. "Anna's got a bead on me somewhere out there."

Dominic smoked rapidly. He dropped my hand and, after some fumbling, lit another cigarette. "What can Anna do?"

"Hey, it's ten minutes," a voice in the crowd, a voice across the street near a bank clock, shouted. He followed that with a blast on a party horn. This set off a chain reaction, until the unbearable noise consumed the street. Drivers mashed their horns.

I talked louder, shouting. "I don't know what twelve years in prison can do to a person. She might be deranged."

"She was already goddamn deranged," Dominic said. He

closed his eyes when a young woman blew a party horn near his head.

"She might be more deranged."

He inched closer so that we heard each other. I backed against the light pole.

"You think she'll try to hurt you?"

"I don't know," I said, "but that came to mind. She's got a reason to do it. Even if she doesn't want to kill me, she'll try something. She'll…I don't know," I said. "Why the hell else would she follow me out here?"

Dominic shook his head. "Have to be pissed to travel a couple thousand miles. Or maybe she wants a job."

I laughed, but it was bitter. "What if the others are out of prison, too?" I asked. "What if her old man is here with her? Or Newt?"

"They both got life," Dominic said. Anna was the only one with a truncated sentence. She had, I assumed, done some snitching. That fact surprised no one, probably not even her old man.

"Five minutes," another voice shouted. "Let's start a countdown."

Dominic said, "That'd be three hundred seconds. Jesus Christ."

No one took up the offer, so the addled stranger did it alone.

"Three hundred. Two hundred and ninety-nine. Two hundred and—"

"Give me a hug," Dom said. He threw away his cigarette and embraced me.

I hugged him close, resting my head on his shoulder. "The year wasn't supposed to end like this," I said. "We're doing so well."

He sighed, but he didn't say anything to that.

"Two minutes!"

We stood that way, hugging under the streetlight, until the countdown ended and 1968 arrived. When midnight struck, and the shouts went up, and bells in a nearby church rang, I kissed Dominic. What the hell else was there to do? His face was cold from the wind, his lips hard and scented with clove.

The car horns kept at it.

CHAPTER THREE

———

The next morning, I had a business engagement. I left Dominic asleep in our apartment and drove to the Desert Botanical Garden at Papago Park. Lack of sleep didn't help my anxiety. I'd stared at the ceiling most of the night, listening to the droning fan on Dom's side of the bed. Now, pushing through what little traffic existed, I stayed in the same place mentally, thinking of nothing except Anna Vogel, and sustained by coffee and cigarettes. The caffeine ratcheted my nerves further. My hands shook.

I went through a lot of scenarios of how things with Anna would play out. I can worry and fret with the best of them. None of the scenarios ended well, so it was an unhealthy exercise. Between waking and arriving at the park's main entrance, I smoked a pack, killed Anna twice, and she killed me a few times. I was bruising myself.

Going on with business was the only thing I could do to stay sane. Otherwise, I'd be locked in the apartment all day, scheming, traipsing through more scenarios. During the night, I'd even considered calling up the Landrums to get in touch with Anna so that I could drive the situation, stay on top of it. I didn't need that, but I wanted a resolution, good or bad. I resisted the urge to telephone.

It was a chilly morning, in the upper fifties, and there weren't many people out given the holiday hangover. I searched for Anna at every stoplight. I didn't find her. This city was much larger than what we'd had in Huntington. I could hide, I told myself.

I pulled the Cadillac into a lot that held three other cars. The park was dead. Beyond the lot stretched intricate walkways and beautiful, sandy gardens of cacti and agave. Gorgeous stone formations rose beyond the expanse, framed by a cloudless sky, red at the horizons. This was one of Dom's favorite spots. We'd walked here and taken in shows at the auditorium many times. I knew the park well, so I'd suggested it for the place of meeting.

I was to speak with a gentleman who called himself Saint Paul. I didn't know his real name or his last name. I only knew he considered himself a mystic, and he believed he communed with extraterrestrials whenever he dropped acid. The drug opened cosmic doorways. He was, he claimed, far out. Saint Paul headed a cult that was batshit about UFOs. His people had all the galaxies mapped out, and they sold slim pamphlets with all the planet names. I owned one. Dom and I attended a Saint Paul "lecture" once. We'd laughed until we cried on the drive home. He frolicked with more aliens than Captain Kirk.

The cult believed in abductions. They wanted to know more about their experiences, but they needed a hypnotist to draw out the details. That's where I entered the picture. I didn't believe a word of it, but their fringe nature gave me an opportunity. Real hypnotists weren't willing to touch crazies like that. I'd been studying up on regression therapy, so I'd planted the idea that I could be of great service to Saint Paul and his people. He did public lectures, so he wasn't hard to get at. I talked to him after one of his engagements, gathered a few names. I got to know his fellow members with some phone calls. I got a book on UFOs and some Philip K. Dick novels from the library. This was a new arena for me, expanding beyond the séance business, but Saint Paul took the bait eagerly. Eagerness is the most important ingredient for me. Eagerness greases the wheels. I let him assume I was a doctor. He called me that. Dom was supposed to put together a fake diploma from a mail-order school in Kansas for me. Kansas seemed believable.

I learned something else in my preliminary talks with Saint Paul and his brethren: one of the cult members was a trust fund baby, and the whole group leaned on this individual for support. That meant the cult had the means to pay well. I planned on giving Saint Paul a nice, healthy number this morning.

In these cases, I only judge men silently. The hypnotist is detached, above such things. A medical *professional*, as it were.

I live to serve.

I opened the door and stood on the asphalt. I wore a suede jacket, which I pulled close to fight the chill breeze. I lit another cigarette, tucked it in the side of my mouth, and strolled toward a sitting area with shade and benches. One of the park workers, cleaning litter from the lot, smiled at me. I waved. Anna was in the back of my mind, but at least I was distracted. I took a seat near a trash can. A bee buzzed around the lid, but otherwise the morning was peaceful. The desert was sublime.

Saint Paul's car came farting into the lot as I finished the cigarette. The jalopy gave me pause. It didn't speak trust funds. I reminded myself that he and his people had concerns up there in the stars, not down here in the dirt. Cars meant nothing to them. Their money went elsewhere, to other concerns, to people like me, perhaps. I laughed, lighting another Chesterfield.

Jesus, I thought, and calmed myself.

The car was a surprise, but Saint Paul was not. He had the look of what one hears about from San Francisco. The nightly news was obsessed with those people and their flowers and guitars and hatred of Vietnam. I wasn't engaged with that scene, but Dom had some friends around town involved in it. Saint Paul wore his hair in hippie fashion, long down to his shoulders and covered at the top by a knitted beanie. The hair was greasy and straight. His pants were burgundy corduroy and his jacket an oversized cardigan of beige. Beneath the sweater he had a striped shirt that fit with a pirate crew. His boots made a lot of jangling noise as he walked. He had the long, slender physique of an adolescent, but he was older than he appeared. He had completed a tour of duty in Vietnam two years prior. Saint Paul was as much into the protest scene as the UFO one, because aliens hated war, too, man. Aliens worried about nuclear weapons.

"Doc Madigan," he said, stepping into the shade.

I stood and shook his hand. "Wonderful to see you again, Saint Paul," I said.

He looked me up and down because he believed in auras. He flashed a mudra—a little sigil with his hands—when he'd finished, a seal of approval.

"Likewise, brother," he said.

Extraterrestrials taught Buddha the mudras, according to Saint Paul. Aliens built the pyramids and Stonehenge, too.

I led him to a bench with a view of the exquisite gardens. Sunlight shone down, teasing out the aroma of the desert.

We sat beside one another. I offered him a cigarette, but he declined.

"Bad for the lungs," said Saint Paul.

You're addicted to heroin, I thought, but I let it go. The man was above irony. I crossed my legs and exhaled a cloud of smoke.

Saint Paul looked out at the lines of cacti. "Beautiful, man," he said. "You know, I don't come out here half as much as I should."

"The desert's the most beautiful thing in the world," I said. "You should always make time for that."

Contemplatively, he nodded.

"Did you celebrate last night?" I asked.

Saint Paul grinned. He removed a pair of glasses with smoked lenses. "We had a visitor," he said. "The ship took four of us along. Didn't you see the lights over the city?"

"Yeah," I said. "I saw that. I had too many drinks to do much about it."

"You know, man, between alcohol and cigarettes, you're gonna kill your body. Your body's a temple, man. You gotta cherish it. You gotta watch what goes in it."

"Uh-huh. Bad vices," I admitted.

He laughed. "I'm not tryin' to be your momma. I do that sometimes."

"Because you're a teacher," I said.

He turned the glasses over in one hand. He liked that. He did a mudra with the other hand, like the Holy Ghost was electricity in his limbs.

"A leader," I continued. "A natural born leader. You and your people fascinate me. What happened last night?"

Saint Paul reclined, stretching his legs.

A woman neared on the sidewalk, walking her dog. She ignored us. The dog didn't. I gave the animal a wink.

"I don't remember too much, man. Bits and pieces. Goddamn if I don't remember those lights, though. They got down in my brain, man. Down where the synapses are firing."

"Yeah," I said, smiling, "that's deep down."

He grew animated then, turning to face me. "I'll tell you one thing I remember. They said this year, 1968, is going to be one of peace. She had a woman's voice—hell, I don't know if that's the way to say it. She had somethin' feminine about her, you know? She always does. She said whatever turmoil, man, the turmoil we face is gonna be obliterated." He obliterated stuff with his hands. "Absolutely going to stun us with peace. No more troubles. None. Like that desert out there all the time. Imagine life like that desert all the time. What do you think about that, my brother?"

"Is Johnson going to end the war?" I asked.

Saint Paul shook his head. "LBJ is gonna get zapped, man. They got heat rays circlin' us right now."

"What about Brezhnev?"

"Dust, man," Saint Paul said. "Same. Zapped."

I flicked away the rest of my cigarette. *Sometimes you must kill for peace*, I thought. *Moral man in an immoral society and all. The aliens understand that.*

"How do you relax?" I asked.

"Grass," he said, matter-of-factly.

"Even after an experience as intense as that?"

"I stay high," he said. "I'm high right now."

"I couldn't tell."

"Trained my eyes to fool the pigs." He flashed his brown eyes. They weren't bloodshot.

"I ask because, with hypnosis, you're going to remember all the details. There won't be gaps. It could prove traumatic."

The thought disturbed him. Regardless of how crazy he sounded, he believed what he said. He believed totally. When he leaned, I poured it on.

"Everything you saw last night, everything you've ever seen, goes down below, down into your subconscious mind. You understand? The memories never leave."

"I do," he said soberly.

"What I do is bring all that out. I need to know you can cope once you hear what is real. We get too many people who find out they don't want to know after they know. By then, it's too late. It's irreversible trauma. The damage is done."

"I dig what you're saying," Saint Paul said. "Man, we want to know, trauma or not."

"As you undergo the hypnosis, we'll tease out all the memories. I'll record it as we go along. Then, when you're ready, you can listen to the tapes yourself."

"Man, Doc, I want you involved."

"I want to help you."

"That's the reason I'm here, man." He looked at me without airs, and I gathered much from his eyes. He was full of hurt, he was a true believer, and he was sophomoric enough to be guided by the sage on the stage. He was a good victim.

"We have to discuss fees," I cautioned.

"Man, whatever you want. But look, I want you to visit the commune. It's up north of here in Snowflake. You know the town?"

I shook my head. I'd never heard of a place called Snowflake.

"I'm all about your energy, man, your aura." He did a quick

mudra that looked arthritic. "I want my people to meet you, Doc. They gotta meet you."

I told him how much money I wanted: $600 for the first round.

He didn't flinch. "You got it, man," he said. "We got that. But you gotta make a mark with my people. We'll pay you to come up and do a session. If we like it, we'll pay for another. If we don't jibe, then that's that. We cut ties. You cool with that, Doc?"

"How far is Snowflake?" I asked.

"Three hours by car. It's up north, man." He mistook my hesitation for displeasure. "I can talk to 'em about coming down here if that's a problem."

It wasn't Saint Paul's intention, but the notion of leaving town was enticing. It excited me, in fact. The excursion would put a lot of miles between me and Anna Vogel. It was an opportunity to hide.

"No, no," I said. "I can make the drive. When?"

"Whenever, man. The sooner the better. We got a helluva lot more than last night to talk about. My people got layers, man."

Through a mask of sincerity, I said, "I believe you. I want to help you. And I'd be lying if I said I wasn't curious."

Saint Paul put on his glasses. "One thing more, Doc: how you feel about 'Nam?"

"I despise it," I said. "It's a criminal war."

"Good. That's real good. We don't want no hawks, man. You're a dove?"

Pure as the driven snow, I thought.

"Peace," I said, "is groovy." I bit my tongue, squirming inside.

"Yeah, man," Saint Paul reflected, "it is, isn't it?"

CHAPTER FOUR

Walking down the hallway to our apartment, I smelled breakfast through the door. Dominic had discovered Julia Child on television a few months prior, and he was working on mastering the French omelet, among other things.

I unlocked the door and stepped inside. The full aroma hit me. Dominic had omelets, bacon, and croissants going in the kitchen. The radio, the speakers of which took up an entire wall in the living room, played the morning news. A window was cracked to let out the charred smell of bacon. The odor went out, the din of traffic came in. Dom stood near the stove, wearing his apron, a copper skillet in his grip. He was buzzed on cocaine. He had that energy, and his eyes said it.

"Hey, watch this," he called.

I walked into the kitchen and leaned against the doorway.

"No spatula," he said, surrounded by steam. He folded the omelet with a flick of the wrist. It was slick. He turned for my reaction, smiling.

I winked at him. "You got it," I said. I'd eaten a lot of eggs for him to master that wrist flip.

He tilted the skillet and the omelet slid onto a plate. He

was finally using the china I'd bought him. Gold leaf rimmed the white porcelain.

"Here. Take this one while it's hot." He began cracking eggs to make another omelet.

I was on edge, so I wasn't hungry. Regardless, I took the plate. He piled on a piece of bacon and croissant and handed me a cup of fresh coffee before I had a seat.

Ardella, our cat, lay on the table, her gray tail hanging over the side. She basked in the smells, her fat tummy bulging. Judging how she looked at me, she expected a piece of bacon. I broke off a crumb and gave it to her.

Our small apartment didn't reach the level of finery that the Duprey residence reached (we had loud neighbors above, below, and on each side), but it was the best home I'd lived in for some time. We had a good neighborhood. I could park on the street and not worry about a smashed window or jimmied lock. Although some people glanced curiously at Dom and I living together, our neighbors minded their business. The older folks thought we were pals. The landlord never questioned us about the arrangement.

We had a living room with stylish shag carpet and wallpaper, a bedroom with a window that opened on a quiet alley, a kitchen, and a bathroom. The ceiling didn't leak. The owner paid for an exterminator to spray once a year. I was content. It was all so mundane and down to earth. Watching Dom at the stove, moving with his apron tied in a bow at the small of his back, I couldn't help but think about Anna Vogel, and I couldn't help but get angry.

She'd take all this away. She was here to do that, to invade a life I'd carefully constructed.

"They already fucked up the ceasefire," Dom was saying.

He folded the omelet, not quite as perfectly as the first time, and then he plated it.

"Huh?" I said, drawn from my thoughts.

"Weren't you listening to the news?"

"Oh," I said. *Vietnam*. That was another of his obsessions. He was too old for the draft, and he was distant from it socially, but he sponged up everything about the war. He attended the protests, usually without me. He considered himself a pundit. "No," I said finally. "I forgot to turn on the radio in the car."

"There was supposed to be a ceasefire for the New Year," he explained.

"Ah. I see."

"A Vietcong attack this morning fucked that."

He shed his apron and joined me at the table. His plate brimmed with bacon. He sat down, adjusted his glasses. He'd brushed back his dark hair without product, so strands hung near his ear. He was gray at the temples. In his robe, he was very domestic and attractive. If not for busy thoughts, I'd be hard for him.

"Westmoreland keeps saying that light at the end of the tunnel shit." Dom shook his head. "He's a lying bastard. He's always lying."

I took a bite of the omelet. It was impressive.

Dom read the look on my face. "Not bad, huh?"

"You made the croissants, too?" I took a bite of the pastry.

"From scratch," Dom said.

"Even more impressive."

He broke off a piece of bacon and slid it to Ardella. She was so lazy she didn't stand. She ate while lying on her side. She was so fat her belly swayed when she walked. She was our baby, though. We couldn't help but spoil her.

"Who's Westmoreland again?" I asked.

"The general."

"Ah. Right." I slid the plate away, unfinished.

A look of severe disappointment crossed Dom's face. "Want me to put on a record?" he asked. "Switch off the news?"

"Yeah," I said. "Do that. I need to talk to you."

He took a large bite of the omelet, and then he stood. He walked into the living room. From the record cabinet, he lifted a Roy Orbison album. It was one I'd played to death, worn smooth. Soon "Only the Lonely" came from the hi-fi. He lowered the volume. Unlike Dom, I was old fashioned when it came to music. I didn't keep up with new artists like he did. I was stuck in the fifties. None of the psychedelic garbage landed with me.

He returned to the table. "Eat more," he told me.

I gave some bacon to Ardella. She purred her thanks.

Dom drank coffee. "Where'd you go this morning?"

I told him about Saint Paul, about the commune in Snowflake, about getting away for a few days. When I finished, Dom was more concerned about how the Botanical Garden looked in January. He missed it. He ignored the point about leaving town.

I took another bite of croissant to satisfy him. My stomach wasn't having it. I gave a piece of the omelet to Ardella. She refused it.

"You have a séance with the Dupreys next week," he reminded me. "They're bringing on a new client."

I'd forgotten that. "Next week" was a couple days away, though. I leaned back and pulled out a pack of cigarettes. I extracted one, lit it.

"Maybe after we've finished with that," I said. "I didn't commit to a date. Saint Paul said whenever."

Dom put his elbows on the table. He blocked Ardella, who'd finally stood, begging. She tried to scavenge from his plate. When he placed the cat on the floor, her tail jittered angrily.

"You can't run away," he said, rising.

I pulled a glass ashtray from the center of the table. I flicked the cigarette. Ardella rubbed my ankle.

"You don't even know what Anna wants," he said.

To say something like that, he had a reserve of optimism I didn't have. I laughed. "I have an idea what she wants."

"But you don't *know*." He crossed his arms. "You can't worry like this about something you don't know for certain."

Watch me, I thought. *I'm good at it.*

"Dom, I was in prison. I know what it does to you. It doesn't straighten you out. It makes you worse. It makes everything worse. Sometimes a lot worse. She's done nothing except plan and plot for twelve years, and she was warped when she went in. I'd say she's totally mindfucked now. She wanted me to find out the way I did. She went to the Landrums. She planned that. She wanted to get in my head."

"It worked."

I flicked ash from the cigarette. "Mm-hm."

"The Landrum part bothers me," Dom admitted. "How do they know her?"

I shrugged. "They talked about her like she was a woman off the street."

"That's utter bullshit," Dom said.

"Yeah." I exhaled smoke. I snuck a piece of bacon under the table to Ardella. "They know her. How they know her, how long—"

"You said he writes an article for skeptics in the *Scientific American*. Maybe she read it. Maybe she wrote to him. Maybe she spent all her time in the prison library, transforming her mind, turning scholar." He smirked.

I'd considered the magazine angle. It made as much sense as anything else I could offer. "Maybe," I said.

"Really, what are you gonna do? You can go but you can't stay away. You gotta come back sometime."

"This," I said. "This right here. I'm going to sit here and fret. Then I'm going to go into the living room and fret. I'll smoke and piss in between. Maybe I'll suck your dick for a distraction."

"What about sleep?"

"Not going to sleep. Can't. I'll stare at the ceiling and fret."

"We got a few barbiturates left. That always puts you to sleep."

I shook my head.

He smiled. "You want me to set up a line for you? We have plenty. I'd like another one." He flicked the edge of his nose with his thumb.

"That's the last thing I need."

"It's the only thing you need. Give you a little verve. Wake you up."

"You know what Saint Paul told me about your war?"

Dom rolled his eyes. "What?" He walked to the living room, switched off the Orbison record, and began searching for another. "This is too depressing," he muttered.

I left the kitchen and joined him. "The mothership told him, just last night, that LBJ is going to be zapped by a heat ray. They're going to step in and end the war. The aliens are tired of our shit. Figured you'd like that."

"I guess that's good news," Dom said. He rifled through the cabinet, flipping through albums. "What about Brezhnev?"

"That's exactly what I asked. He's going to be zapped, too. The aliens take no prisoners."

"Can we put in requests for other people to get zapped? It could be like an oracle in that way. Put names on pieces of paper and burn them."

I pointed at him. "That's not bad," I said. "Who's first against the wall?"

"Well, they got George Rockwell last year, the Nazi, so I'm going with Robert McNamara." He pulled a colorful sleeve from his massive collection of records. "What about you?"

"Anna would be nice," I said, laughing.

Looking back, I saw Ardella on the table, tasting the leftover bacon. I didn't rat her out.

"I've got a show tonight," Dom was saying. "Playing at The Orchard again. Come here. Listen to this. Tell me what you think."

Static gave way to ugly music.

CHAPTER FIVE

For the evening's séance, Adelaide and Florinda secured the use of a mansion outside the city. The home, if one were to call it that, was Baroque and exquisite, full of art, full of long corridors and shadows, sitting like a gothic compound on a flat expanse of bedrock. Sand dunes rose outside the walled gardens. The estate stood far from the highway, so that it was a silhouette against the sky when travelers passed.

The Aguirre family owned the property, and they were old money in Arizona. They claimed to have the blood of conquistadors and Habsburgs, and a lot of the decoration in their home worked to reinforce the claim. Other decor showcased their devotion to the Catholic Church, of which they were a great financial supporter. One of the older Aguirres was a bishop in California, I'd learned. Using the manor came at no cost to me since the Duprey sisters were dear friends with Miss Roma Aguirre. Adelaide arranged everything. I never saw Roma. She remained aloof, although I'd been performing séances at the manor for several years.

It was a bit of a drive from the center of the city, but the atmosphere evoked by the compound made the excursion worthwhile. Ambience did a lot of work for me. My new client would be frontloaded before she ever sat at the table.

Trappings are key in this business, and mood is vital. If I did what I did in the slums, I'd lose from the start. A client would think me cheap, a fraud, capable of no more than the tarot card tricks found on the fair circuit. When I plied my trade at the mansion, though, everything was transformed. Every word meant more. I went from seedy to esoteric, threatening to mysterious, a con man to a medium plagued by the voices of the dead—a role I played well.

Disbelief is a fragile thing.

Days had passed with no sign of Anna, no word from her, no word from the Landrums, so my mind had settled to a degree. I wasn't free of worry, but I felt better, fit enough to work. Dominic asked the pusher he bought from to keep his eyes open for us. He agreed, but we hadn't heard anything from him. The Landrums hadn't spoken to Adelaide since the party when she'd rescinded her invitation to tonight's séance. The couple had faded into the fabric of the city, out of my purview.

After leaving my keys and car with one of the Aguirre servants, then smashing out my cigarette in an ashtray on a pillar, I entered through double doors into the foyer. This was a large square room, two stories high, rimmed at the second story level by a balustrade of sculpted ebony. The walkway behind the railing gave one a fantastic view of the floor, tiled in black-and-white checkerboard fashion, and a closer view of the domed ceiling, painted in the Catholic style of Peter Paul Rubens. Every step echoed in this room. It was meant to make people feel small.

Being cathedral-like, one had to dress properly to enter such a space. I was dressed for the occasion. I might present myself as a medium, but I don't do it by being hokey. Some of the mediums on television look like they stepped out of the Haunted Mansion at Disneyland. Not me. I disarm with class. I wore a bespoke suit, ordered from Benson & Clegg in London. Most of the suits I owned came from Savile Row. Adelaide had insisted on the modern cut, but otherwise the suit was timeless: navy with a little shine on it, a pocket square folded properly, cuff links of gold, a pressed shirt, a striped tie of navy and burgundy knotted with a Windsor, and shoes of black Italian leather. I wore a 24-karat wristwatch from Baume et Mercier, a gift from Dom during our holiday in Geneva. I wore a large Theosophist ring (another gift from Genevieve Blum).

I didn't stand alone for long. A servant, a young woman with white lace in her hair, greeted me, and then she offered to lead me to the room of our event. One wasn't allowed to loiter at the Aguirre estate. I had tried several times before. I'd always wanted to linger and take in the Don and Dona portraits of the main hall, but watching eyes always descended to move me along.

I followed the servant through a corridor of sixteenth century weaponry: Spanish, Ottoman, and Amerindian. Primitive guns and jeweled swords lay in glass cases. We stopped at a door with an iron knocker and the Hernan Cortes coat of arms above the frame, which not so tastefully displayed seven native heads linked by chain.

"They're expecting you, Mr. Madigan," the servant said.

She was too business-like to smile. Some of the servants disliked my presence in the home, and I assumed she was one. I frightened them. They thought I'd invite a haunting, bring in ghosts. I encouraged the belief. That type of publicity never hurts.

She opened the door.

I nodded my thanks.

By design, I was the last to arrive. The room in which we worked held an oblong table built from nineteenth century rosewood, chairs to match, and walls lined with book-filled shelves. This was one of the sublibraries of the estate, with a collection that focused on the history of Spain. The contents of the library matched the corridor outside its walls. A portrait of Philip II, clad in black armor, hung above a fireplace. A map of the Philippines, named after said king, hung on another wall between bookshelves.

A small fire burned in the hearth. It was a chilly night, but the room was comfortably warm. Candles dotted the room.

The new client, Lotte Holden, sat near the head of the table, beside the empty chair that I would occupy. Her husband, Monroe, sat at her right-hand side. He was rigid. She was more receptive to the evening than he. Also at the table were Adelaide, Florinda, and Theda, each of whom smiled at my entrance. The Pyrenees dogs, Thibodeaux and Drucilla, who never missed the opportunity for a car ride, lay tucked in the corner of the room opposite the fireplace, panting but docile.

The guests, including the Holdens, stood in greeting. Solemnly, I nodded at my chorus of supporters. I'd gone to great lengths over several years to convince the Duprey sisters and Theda that their presence aided my abilities, that their energy was special, that their attendance sharpened the conduit through which I communicated with the deceased. Even the dogs, I claimed, were part of this vital energy. To that end, my oracles never missed a séance. Their unwavering belief added to the atmosphere and gave me the proper energy with which to work. It's important that believers outnumber the clients.

I moved around the table to where Mr. and Mrs. Holden

stood. I'd done some fieldwork on the Holden family, and I'd learned some things about their son, but I wanted Monroe and Lotte to talk. That was an important preface to the evening. The more they spoke, the more detailed my communication with their son would be. They held hands as I approached, as if in defense. Their nervousness was palpable. You must put such people at ease. More than anything else, they fear being swindled, made to look like fools. It's a middle-class nightmare. I'm convinced they wake up in the middle of the night sweating about it.

Monroe stood before me stoically, and he looked at me as if I were an insect with pincers. He was difficult to crack. He was tall and successful enough to have some fat on his frame. He wore modern, flamboyant clothes, which told me he lacked confidence rather than possessed it. He was too old to dress the way he did. He wanted to project youth and strength, but he had neither. He wore a suit, pinstriped hideously with red, yellow, and brown. Beneath that he wore a chiffon shirt, opened to reveal his chest. His bell-bottomed pants led to heeled boots rather than proper shoes. His hair was long and parted at the side.

I offered to shake his hand. He reciprocated. Neither of us smiled.

I took Lotte's hand, as well, and here I became gentler. Her fingers were like ice. I gave a reassuring smile. Lotte was a homemaker. She wore a blue dress with orange shoulder pads and a bib fringed by plastic, Native American beads. Her blonde hair was piled a foot high into a bouffant. Crescent-moon earrings dangled from her ears.

Anxiously, she swallowed.

"Very pleased to meet you, Mr. Madigan," she managed to say.

In a moment of inspiration, I did one of the mudras I cribbed from Saint Paul. It was a simple motion of the hand. It didn't match the flamboyance of Monroe's suit.

Lotte watched my hand, and then she looked me in the eye.

"What does that mean?" she asked.

"Your grandfather was British," I said. "I'm getting that sense. He lived in India, though, for a time."

She nodded. "That's true," she said. "How—"

"That was a mudra," I said. I repeated the gesture. "I don't know what it means. It just came to me. I was compelled to do it. Did your grandfather have a connection with Hinduism, Mrs. Holden?"

"He was part of the liberation front there," she said. "That's why he left the UK and came here."

"I see. I'm sorry I can't tell you what it means. Maybe your grandfather will tell us tonight. He was a deeply knowledge-able man." I paused, let the gravity settle. "I daresay he was a great man."

Lotte inhaled slowly. She blinked rapidly.

She'd be cake, I decided. She gave with the first push.

I turned to Monroe.

"Thank you for doing this," he said.

"You're here for Mrs. Holden," I said, staring hard into his eyes. "Not for yourself."

Monroe broke the stare, glancing at Lotte. "I'm keeping an open mind," he said. He took a deep breath, gathering himself.

"Please have a seat," I said.

Everybody sat and pulled their chairs closer to the table. After all were in place, I took my seat. Behind me, the dogs breathed heavily, loudly through their mouths, asleep. I didn't mind it. The noise, always unexpected to the guests, aided with misdirection.

With a parlor trick, I extinguished the candles in the room with a wave of my hand. One by one, the flames blinked out, leaving the fireplace as the only light. An orange glow crossed the table, jittering. Shadows and streaks of firelight touched our faces. A hush settled over the room. I let the quiet extend for several seconds as anticipation built. Then, to unbalance the Holdens, I looked at Monroe. He found my eyes in the darkness.

"I want Mr. Holden to sit here," I said. I gestured at the seat to my left, presently unoccupied. He didn't question why, but I explained, regardless. "As we join hands," I said, "I must channel both energies. You have distinct auras. You'll engage differently with what occurs tonight. I need to feel both."

When Monroe had reseated himself, I urged everyone to join hands. I took Lotte's into my right, and I grasped Monroe's with my left. My real reason for splitting the couple was simple: I wanted to isolate his negativity, to remove him from his wife so that I could work on her properly. She was as good as alone now.

It was as I channeled one of my spirit guides—Saint Germain was on tap for the night—

that an unexpected knock came at the library door. Three quick raps. Lotte jumped out of her skin. Monroe flinched. I kept calm, although my mind ran. Adelaide's face turned crimson with rage at the far end of the table.

She broke the circle and stood.

I unclasped Lotte and Monroe but stayed seated. I attempted a noble bearing.

Adelaide stepped to the door. The dogs, awake and alert, watched her closely.

The insistent knocking continued with three more raps.

Adelaide turned to the group. "I apologize," she said in a clipped voice. She opened the door a crack, allowing the bright lights of the corridor to pour inside, kicking a hole in the atmosphere. She slipped through the opening, and then she shut the door behind.

The room pulsed with silence.

I looked to Lotte. "The connection can be rekindled," I promised. "We haven't yet begun."

She nodded, relieved.

Inside, I was more worried than angry. The Aguirre servants wouldn't interrupt because of ignorance or rudeness. Adelaide would see them fired for such behavior. There had to be an emergency to warrant the intrusion. I thought about Dominic. He was doing a show tonight in one of the seedier barrios. I'd warned him against it, asking him to accompany me here instead. He was the only one who knew I was a fraud, so he worked wonders when he joined the circle. He'd insisted on the show, though. He thought himself an artist. One day I hoped to see him smash his instruments.

When Adelaide returned, the servant followed her into the room. Adelaide looked as puzzled as she was angry. I couldn't read the servant's face.

"Mr. Madigan," Adelaide said. "Will you please step into the hall for a moment?"

Florinda and Theda looked at one another.

"What is this?" Florinda asked her sister.

Adelaide urged her to be calm.

"This is not the norm," Theda reassured the Holdens.

I walked out of the library. Adelaide, the servant, and I stood alone with the weapons surrounding us. I shut the door. Quietly, I asked for an explanation. It was the same servant who guided me to the library at the beginning of the night—the one with white lace in her hair. She liked me less now than she did then. She looked at me emphatically.

"Sir, there is a mad woman at the front gate. She is insisting upon being allowed inside. We refused her, but she is *climbing* the gate, sir."

"How, pray tell, does this involve dear Royce?" Adelaide asked.

"Madam, the woman asks for a 'Royce Pembrook.' I only assumed she meant Mr. Madigan."

"Did you telephone the police?"

"The constabulary is on their way."

"We have to cancel tonight. I'll reschedule with the Holdens," I said.

"What is the woman's name?" Adelaide asked, indignant, crimson moving from her face into her neck.

I looked at the servant for a response, but I knew the answer to that.

CHAPTER SIX

Royce, no. Stop!" Florinda shouted.

I stopped short of the foyer and turned. Florinda sprinted after me, leaving Theda, Adelaide, and the Holdens behind. I took out a cigarette, put it in my mouth, remembered I couldn't smoke here, and then put it up again. I was fumbling with the pack when Florinda reached me. She held Drucilla by the leash. The dog wore a leather harness to keep her in check. She squirmed and pulled, wanting to rush past us to the front door.

Shouting emanated from the courtyard. The police had yet to arrive. The servants were trying to deal with the intruder.

"What are you doing?" Florinda asked. "You're not going to step out there and get yourself hurt by some zealot."

Theda and Adelaide came down the hall, both frightened, concerned. Adelaide held Thibodeaux on his leash. He was a stoic guardian, his face alert.

"It's not what you think," I said.

When she neared, Theda asked, "Who is that woman, Royce? Is that her yelling out there?"

I nodded. I waited for Adelaide, then said, "I want the three of you to remain here."

"We can sic Drucilla and Thib on her," Florinda offered.

"Is that the Landrum woman from the party?" Theda asked. "What a perfectly heinous creature."

"I'm going to step out and defuse the situation," I said. I'd thought about how I'd phrase things if this ever happened, but I couldn't muster any of the speeches I'd rehearsed. I'd cooked up some doozies during sleepless nights. Now my tank was dry.

"She's," I said, grasping for delicacy, "mentally disturbed. It isn't the Landrum woman. Her name is Anna Vogel, and she is a lunatic. She believes things about me that are untrue. That's as plainly as I can put it. The police will be here soon enough, but I can't allow one of the servants to be injured on my behalf. I simply can't do that. If she wants to speak with me, then I'll talk to her."

"She's that dangerous?" Adelaide asked. "Royce, no."

"She traveled 2,000 miles for this. Now she's scaling a gate."

"Please reconsider," Adelaide begged. "The Aguirres will find new servants. They're replaced easily enough."

"Oh, you're horrid," Theda said.

"Remain here," I repeated. I looked at Florinda specifically. "I know what you're thinking. Don't do it."

"Our driver carries a gun," Florinda said.

"Really?" I asked.

"Oh, dear lord," Theda said.

"Florinda!" Adelaide protested.

"Well, he does. It's like a cannon in his glove box. I've seen it."

"She gave it to him," Theda said. "Don't let her fool you."

"Perhaps, I did," Florinda said.

I disengaged and hurried through the foyer. Footfalls reverberated to the domed ceiling. Adelaide made certain Florinda and Theda stayed behind, as requested. I was grateful for that. The dogs pulled on their owners, but otherwise they behaved. The Holdens stayed in the library, confounded. If they saw police, their business was lost to me.

"Console Lotte," I called over my shoulder.

I pushed through the double doors and emerged onto the stone steps of the estate. The moon was bright over the desert, and the air was dry and cold. There was no traffic, no lights on the distant highway. On one hand I was a ball of nerves, on the other I was desperate for release. Impatience is a weakness of mine, so I had to act. I couldn't stand hiding from Anna any longer. I'd been tortured for days. I'd be tortured for days to come. This was the beginning of a resolution, I reassured myself.

If she doesn't kill you.

If she doesn't kill me, yes.

I saw Anna. Absurdly, she stood in a ring of uniformed servants, beneath an oil lamp in one of the agave beds. When she saw me on the stairs, illumined by the floodlight over the main entrance, she stopped fighting. She quit shouting, and she stood erect, as if conscious of the pride of her posture. She straightened her shirt, repositioned her trousers, and put a palm to her disheveled, platinum hair. Her chest heaved with rapid breaths. Likewise, the servants stopped their maneuvering. In a moment that I won't forget, everything fell under the spell of a hush.

Across the divide, Anna and I stared at one another. There were twelve years in that moment. *More than that.* I'd known Anna since the forties, after all. We'd slummed through the fair circuits. We'd suffered together. We'd made money together. I also killed her boyfriend, saw her husband imprisoned, and stole twelve years of her life. The disparity couldn't be undone. We were creatures with vastly different fortunes, and both fortunes were of our making. Anna blamed me. I blamed Anna.

I'd imagined that she'd want to kill me, and I'd want to kill her, but those thoughts weren't foremost. It was a bizarre moment, in fact—one of toxic nostalgia. I was in 1956. I was in Cincinnati. Neither angry nor sad, I only existed. The feeling encompassed me.

I gathered myself. I moved to the bottom of the steps. The servants watched my approach, startled at my appearance, and Anna slipped from their confinement. Her trousers were ripped above the knee, either from scaling the gate or taking a fall. She was very thin, gaunt around the neck, and she looked much older than her fifty years. An inch of gray roots preceded the platinum in her hair. Dirt tattooed her skin, and I wondered if she'd hitched rides across the country to get here. She looked like one of the bag ladies who loiter downtown.

"Royce?" she asked. She laughed a little. Perhaps the absurdity struck her. Perhaps the disparity of fortunes did. "Royce, is that you?"

I nodded. "Hello, Anna," I said. I put up my hand to stop her advance. I didn't want her too close. I recalled a time in a hotel room when she'd pulled a Beretta on me.

She stopped. Anna looked like she had no possessions at all, let alone a gun.

I motioned for the servants to stop, as well. They were prepared to tackle the woman from behind and kneel on her back.

I made things as plain as possible, conscious of the servants in earshot.

"What do you want?" I asked.

Anna's anger and insanity were wound tightly, compressed

into a dense seed that lit her eyes. It was the only life in her gaze. Even without the blustering and shouting, there was an air of danger about the woman. Prison had worked on Anna. The pain of that life warped her anger, spat her out as this thing that stood before me.

On the surface, Anna willed herself to be calm. She didn't cry, and she didn't shout.

"I wanted to look at you," she said.

A mix of drugs, malnutrition, and hardship gave her a cadaverous appearance, especially with the floodlight putting shadows in the hollows of her eyes and jaws. I'd once compared her to Helen Chandler, Mina in *Dracula*. She was only a shell of that person. She looked like Mina drained of blood.

It's difficult to explain the trauma triggered by the sound of Anna's voice. Old pain flooded me. The emotions nearly made me retreat up the steps, but I stood my ground.

"I don't want you in my life," I said directly. "I don't want to see you again, Anna. Ever."

"You have no choice," Anna said. She spoke with no emotion, her voice flat. She stepped closer.

I smelled her. She had the rot of the homeless on her clothes. She was gutter trash.

Anna looked at the mansion, scanning the lighted windows, the high roof, the gables, all silvered by moonlight. She then looked me over, lingering on the fine suit, the golden watch.

"You're not doin' so fuckin' bad, old boy," she said.

"Tell me what you want."

"I already told you. I just wanted to look at you."

"You've had your look," I said. "That's it?"

Anna smiled, and I sensed some of her willpower slipping as she did. Turbulence surfaced in her eyes.

"That's it. Don't you wanna have a look at me, too?" She laughed. The façade of her control wavered. "I ain't got any fuckin' jewelry like you. I had to sell it."

I shook my head.

"You hoped I'd die in there, didn't you?" she spat.

"Yes," I said quietly.

Again, the tight smile. She calmed herself by breathing, something I imagined the penitentiary psychiatrist taught her.

"Marvelous cologne," she said, smelling the air. "Old boy, I'm gonna make you fuckin' miserable. I'm gonna pull you back down here with me where you belong until you got fuck all." Anna admired the Aguirre home. "Not here. You don't belong here anymore than I do. You're a fraud. You fuckin' asscock. I'm gonna make sure everyone in town fuckin' knows it, too."

I checked my swell of rage. It had been a long time since I'd given in to the urge of violence. The instinct waited impatiently at my fingertips, waited to be embraced. *Not here* was correct, although not in the way Anna intended it. I wouldn't be violent at the Aguirre estate, not in front of the Dupreys, because Royce Madigan was a cultured man. He was considerate, conscientious, caring. He was incapable of such things as brutality.

Royce Pembrook, however, was very capable.

The siren of a police cruiser reached us. The car neared on the highway. The lights came into view, and one of the servants sprinted toward the front gate to open it manually.

"You never had patience," I taunted Anna. "Imagine what a little patience would have done for your life."

Anna looked at me, and her face relaxed. "You're still you," she said. "Still a smug fuckin' prick that thinks you're up there and everyone else is down here. That's what I really wanted to know."

I turned to go back up the steps. The cruiser, with siren quieted, rolled down the driveway between the gardens.

"I don't want to see you again, Anna," I said. "This was your first mistake."

"Count on a few more, old boy," she said.

One of the cops gestured for me to go inside. The young men in uniform approached Anna from behind. They moved with the delicacy one brings to stepping around lunatics. Anna began to kick and shout, and I realized that the behavior was fake. She had more control than she pretended to have. She wanted to play up intoxication. She had her eyes on the drunk tank. It was an excuse she'd tucked in her pocket.

Why here? I thought. *Why now?*

The silhouettes of Adelaide, Florinda, and Theda at the front entrance answered that question. Anna wanted to be seen by my keepers. The three women had watched the drama unfold. I wondered how much of it they had heard. I petted the dogs when I approached. I said nothing.

Behind me, the officers stuffed Anna into the cruiser. The door slammed shut, muffling her voice.

"The Holdens gathered their things," Adelaide said. "They're leaving."

"I suppose they have no interest in rescheduling?" I asked. It was rhetorical. I knew my reputation with Lotte Holden was tainted. When people are wary of fraud, you can't have the police show on the horizon.

Adelaide shook her head.

I turned. One of the cops was hailing me from the bottom of the steps.

"The lady says this belongs to you, sir," he said. He held a torn piece of paper, a sliver.

I accepted it without thanks. There was a telephone number scrawled on the paper, nothing more.

CHAPTER SEVEN

I sat on the sofa in the dark, petting Ardella. She was curled in my lap, purring. The cat sensed something was off in my manner. She acted this way when I was sick. The television supplied the only glow in the room. The volume was low. An old movie, *Cat People*, played on a rerun of *Big 9 Chiller* with Dr. Scar. Touched by Ardella's concern, I left the movie on for her sake. She liked the noise, and I assumed the subject matter wasn't unappealing. The panther in the zoo scene struck her fancy. She watched it with pricked, alert ears.

The window was lifted, allowing in street noise and chilly air. I had a glass of Bombay gin on the side table, and it waited beside an ashtray that needed emptying. I'd cleared a pack of Chesterfields while waiting on Dominic to arrive home. I'd swallowed a barbiturate to relax. Nothing lessened my tension. Every footfall in the hallway had me anxious.

Of course, my mind went dark with scenarios. I wondered if Ruben Graf had been released from prison like Anna. What if Graf confronted Dom just as Anna confronted me? What if Graf, cloaked in an alley, waited on Dom outside the venue tonight?

I scratched the inside of Ardella's ear, and she tilted her

head with pleasure. I took a long drink of the gin. The warmth of drunkenness was like a mask sliding from my face.

When Dominic's key entered the door, and the locks grinded open, I was grateful to the point of being emotional. A lot of feelings welled up inside. Tears formed where I'd dammed them before. I'd yet to vent the emotions of the night. I'd resisted the temptation to unload on the Dupreys and Theda.

Dom, puzzled by the scene, switched on a lamp. He found me a pale ghost in the dark. My suit was crumpled in the bedroom, and only a white T-shirt and briefs remained.

I placed Ardella on the cushion at my side and stood. The cat stretched.

Dom put his guitar case on the floor.

"What happened?" he asked.

I couldn't put into words how grateful I was that he was safe, so I took him into my arms and hugged him. He gripped me, raising his head so I could rest my face on his shoulder. He kissed my hair. When I finally let him go, he led me to the couch. Sweetly, Ardella climbed into my lap again.

Dominic disappeared into the kitchen, and then he returned with two copitas filled with sherry. Unlike me, he had a sweet tooth when it came to alcohol. I took the glass anyway. He sat beside me on the sofa. He smelled strongly of beer and grass. His greased hair had come undone. He watched the television screen for a moment, sipping the sherry, fighting exhaustion.

"Simone Simon," he said, smiling. "You like this one?" he asked Ardella.

"It's her favorite," I said.

Dom put his hand on my knee. He wasn't wearing his gold rings, I noticed. They were still arranged on the vanity in our bedroom. He never wore them to his shows—affluence hurt his image.

"What happened?" he asked. His voice was soft, even if forced. I knew it didn't reflect the turmoil and worry he felt. Dom always tried to be strong for me.

I told him. In what felt like an unbroken stream, I told him everything that occurred, and I told him everything that didn't (even my worries about him in the barrio).

He smoked a clove cigarette, sipped sherry, and listened.

When I finished, I asked him how his show had gone. He had planned to introduce an original song tonight. The question was a pathetic attempt to include him. Dom pushed it aside with a shrug.

With him home and safe, the barbiturate started working on my brain. Heavy fatigue spread through my limbs.

Dom was shaken by what I told him, but he tried to be level. "The police have her now," he reassured me.

I was so tired I put my head on his shoulder. "That won't last," I said.

"It might. You can press charges."

"For what?"

"Maybe Roma Aguirre could."

"More like she'll bar me from using her home, and that'll be the end of it. I doubt they want to involve police. It'll make the paper as it is. Half of them already think I'm a worshipper of devils."

"They won't bar you. Addy won't allow it."

"Addy's patience is wearing thin. Dom, I humiliated her tonight. You don't humiliate people like that."

"Now I know that isn't true," Dominic said. "She'd go to the end of the earth to help you. She adores you, Royce. Even if she is embarrassed, it won't last."

"You really think so?" I asked.

The movie ended, an American flag filled the screen for the station's sign off, and the national anthem played in brass.

"Goddamn fascists," Dom muttered. He stood and switched off the set. The screen blinked to a point and went dark.

I rested on my side, positioning my head on the arm of the couch.

Dom walked to the hi-fi. He sipped sherry and rummaged through the record cabinet below. Finally, he said, "Addy and Florinda would kill for you."

I don't think he meant it the way it settled in my mind. Regardless, a root grew from the idea.

"Would you do that for me?" I asked.

He drained the last of the sherry and put the copita aside.

"Sure I would," he said. "If you were ever in trouble, I'd kill for you in a second."

The words were too flippant, too quickly formed to be real. Dominic talked about killing like a man who had never shed blood, and I knew he expected me to do the same. There was no seriousness in such talk. Like the Dupreys, he believed that innocence lived in me.

Anna knew me in a way that Dominic did not. I'd never brought myself to tell him the truth. It would always be a stain on our relationship, one I knew, and one he didn't. I maintained a lie we had shared from the start. To Dom, I was always a victim, always the prey. The longer the lie went on, the more I was determined to bury it. I'd never even told him about my grandfather's death. Dom still believed my mother was a murderer.

"I'd kill for you, too," I said, and I intoned it as he did—as if these were only words, as if this meant nothing.

When Ardella stood to reposition herself, I stretched my legs, covering the length of the couch. Tired of my shit, she jumped to the floor. The cat sauntered toward her bowl in the kitchen.

"You're the gentlest man I've ever known," Dominic said. In the lamplight, he slid a record from its sleeve. He placed it on the turntable and lifted the needle. "I don't believe you have it in you to hurt anybody."

"But you do?" I asked. My tone wasn't one of challenge. It was soft, tired, curious.

"If pushed hard enough, yes. Not you, though, Royce."

"I lie for a living," I reminded him. "My ethics are warped."

"Who's hurt by that? It might be lies, but you only bring comfort to people who need it." He started the record and returned to the sofa. He knelt until his face was level with mine. "It's no different than a priest to me. Hey, you remember that little radio you used to carry?"

I nodded. It was still around, hidden in one of the junk drawers. The radio had stopped working long ago, but I couldn't trash it.

"You remember we had dinner in your hotel room, and you had the radio playing?"

"Yes."

"That was our first date."

"You stole soup from the kitchen." I laughed.

Dom laughed, too. "This is one of the songs that played."

The Chordettes came softly through the speakers. A corny old song from a different age. That song didn't exist into today's world. One couldn't listen to it unironically anymore.

"I remember," I said.

He kissed my forehead. "Try to sleep. I'll watch the door."

"Dom, I love you."

He gave me a deeper kiss. "I love you more," he said. "We'll get through it. Don't be scared." Dom took my sherry from the table and began to work on it. He thought I was asleep, but I watched him for a while longer. He switched off the lamp and brooded in the darkness.

CHAPTER EIGHT

F lorinda and Drucilla greeted me at the door. Behind her, the apartment was dark except for three points of candlelight. The hi-fi was off, the atmosphere subdued. Thibodeaux was stretched on the divan, snoring, unbothered by my intrusion.

"Where's Addy?" I asked, stepping inside. As usual, the place was roasting. I removed my coat.

There was a great deal of stress in Florinda's gaze. Shadow hid the rising color of her face. "Ian called again," she said. Momentarily, she was vulnerable and upset, very much unlike the woman I knew. Ian Duprey was her brother. He was also the man who clutched the purse strings in the family.

"He telephoned?" I pried, hanging my coat on a hook of silver. I straightened my tie.

"He pushed his way in here about an hour ago. For once, I was thankful you were delayed. I never want you to suffer his arrogance, Royce. It's unbearable. Addy left with him so that we could have our session. She'll keep him away. He wouldn't have allowed this, you know."

"Why wouldn't Ian have allowed it?"

Florinda balled her fists. "Because he is a controlling, intolerable prick. He lords over us when he is here. He lectures us, Royce. Imagine it. He threatens to stop our 'allowances' unless we do as he says. God, he's just like our father. How I wish his heart would finally kill him, too."

"There are ways to hasten that," I muttered. "He lectures you about what? About me?"

Florinda dismissed the idea.

Yes, I thought, *he does*.

"Don't be silly," she said, but I knew she didn't think it silly. Nor did Ian.

I stared at her until she was uncomfortable.

He heard about the Aguirre incident, I thought, but I left it alone.

"You need a drink to relax," I said finally. "Stress blocks me. You know that."

"He simply rattled me is all," said Florinda. "I'll recover."

We crossed the room to the bar. Three cubist miniatures lined the outcropping, edging the ceiling. A tall wax candle burned in a shaft of silver. The light flickered.

The penthouse was, I thought, *a lonely place when Addy was gone, too quiet, too large, too empty.*

"Everyone is pissing me off lately," she said. "Speaking of, have you heard more from the nasty Landrums? I could have killed them." She retrieved the gin. She poured a shot. Her hand was shaking.

"Go ahead," I said. "You need it."

Florinda drank. Her face relaxed.

I patted Drucilla's heavy head. "I was hoping you would kill them. Or that you would," I said to the dog.

Florinda snorted. "Would you return the favor?"

I let that go. "Will you tell me something?" I asked.

"Yes. What is it?" She looked at me sincerely from the edge of candlelight.

"Is Addy upset with me about the other night? Is that why she isn't here? Be honest."

Florinda poured another drink. "She's upset but not with you. She was embarrassed, of course. She spoke to Roma. She doesn't blame you, Royce. Nothing could be further from the truth."

"Do you blame me?"

"I wouldn't have you here if I did, would I? It's simple enough to cancel plans, dear."

I smiled my thanks and tried to shrug off the heavy feeling.

"Do you have everything set up?" I asked.

Florinda downed another shot, and this one steadied her hand. "With a new addition," she said. "Too bad Addy isn't here to gloat. She purchased it. Come along."

I followed Florinda and Drucilla past Thib toward a shelf of books in the far corner of the room. Here a table and three chairs were arranged for the séance. A fat candle burned at the center of the table, but otherwise it was bare. The wood was old and cut crudely, full of vibrations but out of place in the modern surroundings. A pair of Ming vases served as evocative pillars, closing in the tableau. Two portraits, finely rendered on canvas, of the Great Pyrenees siblings book-ended the elegant library.

Florinda fetched a book by the spine. She handed the leather-bound volume across to me. It was the fruit of an idea I'd been playing with, building belief in the Duprey sisters, a belief that they had the power inside to communicate with the dead. The power needed to be unlocked, I preached. I held *Isis Unveiled: A Master-Key to the Mysteries of Ancient and Modern Science and Theology* by Madame Blavatsky. The text was a cornerstone of theosophy. *Bunk*, as Karl Landrum would put it. Maybe, but I needed the sisters to unlearn a lifetime of Catholicism. Theosophy was the crowbar.

"'There is no religion higher than truth,'" Florinda quoted proudly.

I let my stress drop and played the character I'd trained a decade to play. She wanted that, and I needed it.

"You're growing mentally," I said. "You're kindling a dormant ability. It'll come in time. I want you to read this."

"I have been, little by little."

"I want you to know it. Know it thoroughly."

Florinda nodded.

"There will come a day when you don't need me to cross the veil. You won't need me to take your hand and guide you. You'll know the way."

"I doubt that, Royce."

"Don't. I want you to believe."

Drucilla curled on the floor, sighing. She drew deep breaths, courting sleep.

"Please take a seat," I said.

Florinda did as she was told. I put the book on the shelf, and then I sat opposite her. I stared through the haze of candlelight. Our target of communication, as it always was, was Reginald Leigh, Florinda's husband of eighteen years. He had been dead for nine years. Florinda and I spoke with him weekly. He was amusing, romantic, and mean in turns. I learned what I could about him and made up the rest.

I reached across the table, one arm on each side of the candle, and took Florinda's hands. They were dry and cold but steady. We locked eyes over the dot of flame. She and I always played the ritual simple. With her, I didn't need the theatrics. The quiet of the room settled around us, as did the heat.

"I'm going to count backwards from twenty," I said. "In that time, I want you to forget Ian, forget the Landrums, forget Anna, drop any barrier, and I want you to focus instead on an image of Reginald. I want that form to be solid and real in your mind, as real as it is in your heart."

Florinda nodded.

"Close your eyes," I said.

She did. Her jowls quivered.

I counted down from twenty, slowly. Fifteen, slower. Ten, slower.

Her breathing calmed. Her pulse calmed.

Five, slower.

"Reggie," I said, using Florinda's pet name for a man I never knew. "Reggie, your darling wife—"

Thibodeaux jumped from the divan, cutting me off, releasing a tremendous bark that rimmed the apartment. He was a sheepdog keeping wolves from the firelight in that moment, fresh from sleep and primitive.

Florinda opened her eyes, jarred from the spell I wove.

Drucilla lifted and trotted toward the line of windows on the far wall. She, too, barked, deep and guttural. The dogs, their heads above a sill, stared into the night, bristling, tails high and alert.

Florinda got to her feet.

"Just sit and relax," I said. "It's no more than a plane flying over."

"No," she said. "They don't bark unless it's serious. Pyrs take their duty as guardians quite seriously, Royce."

"Sit," I said, and realized I'd lost control over the woman.

She ignored me, walking to the windows.

My frustration grew. I looked down to find my chest

moving with rapid breaths. I knew what the disturbance was just like Florinda knew. I trailed her to where the dogs stood firm.

A distant shouting, a singular voice, came through the glass. Florinda looked at me. I lifted the window, poked out my head, and looked down ten stories to the busy street.

In a repeat of the Aguirre incident, Anna stood in traffic, shouting at the heavens, shouting for me, losing her mind.

Snippets alone reached high through the blare of the city.

"Fucker won't let me in, Royce, but I know you're there," I heard.

I felt Florinda's bulk on my back then, as she strained to see over my shoulder. The dogs, too, crowded us in the window.

"It's that mad woman," said Florinda. "Jesus God, she's calling you into the street like it's a knife fight. It's abhorrent, Royce. Oh, people are watching."

People were, in fact, leaning from the windows, watching the lunatic theater.

Florinda backed from the window. The dogs remained on each side of me.

Fake. Liar. Cheat. Con. Murderer, Anna spouted.

She followed me here, I thought. She stood near where Dom and I had greeted the New Year. *Was she in the crowd, watching that night, too?*

I hung out the window, looking downward, deciding, plotting. A quiet rage grew inside, tempering my panic.

"It's humiliating," Florinda was saying. She went to an oil painting of Reginald on the wall. "I'm so sorry, Reggie. This is absurd." She switched on the lights, closing the séance, chasing the ghost. "Is he in limbo now?" she asked. "Had he already crossed the veil?"

I pulled a cigarette from my pocket. I put it unlit in my mouth and let it hang there.

Drucilla growled deep in her throat.

"Shall I call the police?" Florinda asked from the bar. She downed more gin.

"It isn't necessary," I said.

Florinda didn't hear me. "I'll call Addy," she said. "She's at Ian's. She needs to know."

Several blocks away, a siren pulsed, running lights, closing the distance.

Anna shredded her lungs with a final scream, and then she ran into the night.

Murderer, she'd said.

I bit the cigarette, tasting shards of tobacco, watching traffic unsnarl.

———

CHAPTER NINE

At a gas station on the edge of Route 60, I paced the cracked pavement from a pay phone to the Cadillac. It was a cool, dry day, despite the beating sun. We were on a lonely, tumbleweed stretch. Dom had the passenger's side window rolled down, his elbow on the sill. He was licking an Astro Pop.

"Florinda finally answered," I said. "I let her know we'd be out of town a few days."

"How'd she take it?" Dom asked.

"She told me to call Karl Landrum."

I leaned on the rear door. I removed the cellophane from a new pack of Chesterfields. I'd bought a carton and Dom's candy along with a tank of gas from an asshole attendant. I took out a cigarette and lit it. A nice breeze moved in from the desert.

A bell at the station rang when a car rolled to a stop at one of the pumps. The attendant walked out of his shed, eyed us in the side lot for a second too long, and then went to the customer. A green billboard for Kool cigarettes and an orange Gulf sign stood above. The highway stretched into the distance. The two-lane blacktop roiled.

Dominic opened the door and stood. He stretched his

back until it popped. We'd been on the road for an hour, heading north to Snowflake. I had directions from Saint Paul. Dom wore a Hawaiian shirt with short sleeves and a fat collar, and he had on sunglasses with yellow lenses. It was a style he gravitated toward lately, but I wasn't a fan. His shirts were tacky. It was better than the hippy shirts he wore for shows, however, so I didn't tell him. Dom didn't care either way. He worked on the lollipop.

Irritably, I said, "Landrum's been calling their penthouse morning, noon, and night."

"Saying what?" Dom asked.

"Whatever Anna tells him to say." I took a drag. "He's keeping her out of jail, man."

He shook his head.

"I'm guessing he dropped Anna at the Aguirre place. Then on the street outside Florinda and Addy's. He's shuttling her around, following me."

"I wondered how the hell she got out there," Dom said. "She sure as shit didn't walk."

"With the calls, he's laying out my story—at least the way Anna sees it. He had information on my time in Mansfield this morning. The fraud charges. All that. My mother. He wants to turn Addy and Florinda against me."

Dom grimaced. "Where would he get that information?"

"Anna knows all that. She's feeding it to him."

"What's Florinda think?"

I exhaled. "She doesn't believe it, thank God. She thinks they're cranks. She said Addy's depressed, though. She's holing up in her bedroom. She even locked out Thibodeaux."

"They're more than cranks. They're fuckin' insane."

"Anna maybe. I think the Landrums are pretty level."

"Then why go after you?" Dominic asked.

I gestured with the cigarette. "That I don't know. I can't remember ever having met them. Could be someone is putting them up to it."

"Maybe you *should* call Karl."

"I walked over here with the intent of begging another dime. I keep changing my mind. It could make me look desperate. I don't want to grovel."

The attendant was pointing at us, talking to the driver at the pump. A fit of laughter passed between the men. Following the joke, the car angled and pulled away from the pump. It moved in an arc that positioned the driver's side to us. It was an old beater with rusted-out holes in the body. The window was down, and a man with a severe buzz cut looked at us.

Dom and I turned.

The driver was young white trash. The car kept rolling, but it was only a crawl.

"Look at those pretty boys," the man said. A large, sweaty woman sat next to him in the passenger seat. Egregiously, she laughed. "Get out to San Francisco where you belong, fancy boys! This is still God's country, queers!" He spun his back wheels and kicked dust. He didn't stick around. He was gone on the highway before we reacted. He left a cloud of exhaust and dirt in his wake.

I looked at Dom. He was more embarrassed than angry.

"We need to stay in the city," he said, as if that were a haven. He looked pathetic, holding the Astro Pop, deflated. That image got in my mind and took hold. I'd known Dominic a long time. He was from a hick town where it was shameful, sinful, and deplorable to be with another man. Try as he might, he'd internalized some of that loathing. The Bible's a tricky thing to wash out when you're beaten over the head with it as a child. A touch of guilt mixed with his embarrassment.

I'd tried to fight that guilt out of him, but it was always there, deep below. He couldn't escape his upbringing.

Seeing that look on his face, coupled with the stresses of Anna, I went red with rage. I threw my unfinished cigarette on the ground and stomped it.

"Don't say that," I told him. "Don't—" I don't even know what I wanted to admonish him for, so I stopped.

He started to get back in the car.

"We can go where we—" I stopped when I saw the gas-station attendant approaching.

Dom had the door open.

"Get in and close the door," I said. "Get the window up."

Dom watched the attendant. "Let's just get outta here," he said, fear in his voice.

"I've taken enough shit this week," I said. I experienced the same urge I felt while on the Aguirre steps watching Anna. It had been a long time. Suddenly, I needed it like a fiend. "Get that blackjack out of the glove box."

"I don't like you fairies loiterin' on my property," the attendant said.

He was a younger man, twenties, with two days growth of beard. Arizona has hicks, too, and he was one. That realization was a big disappointment I had when moving out West. Every place has hicks on the fringes, I'd concluded. There was no escaping them. He wore a trucker hat with Copenhagen emblazoned across the foam. Curly hair peeked from the hat and covered his neck. His hands were black with oil. He wasn't carrying a weapon. The closest thing he had at hand was a large ring of keys hooked to his belt loop.

"Let's leave, Royce," Dominic begged.

"Give me the goddamn blackjack," I spat.

Shaken, bruised by my tone, Dom popped open the glove

box. He rifled around and pulled free a metal bar the size of his palm encased with leather. He handed it over. I'd had that blackjack for two decades. I knew how to use it. It was the same one I'd used to open the head of Anna's boyfriend.

The attendant stopped ten feet from me. He balled his fist, and then he pointed to the highway.

"You got what you wanted. Now get in your car and get your candy asses outta my lot."

I was too angry to be scared. I saw nothing but red. A lot of old trauma washed over me, and I let it run.

"Did you hear what that man said to us?" I asked.

"Hear? You dumbass, cock-sniffin' sonnuva bitch, I gave him a discount for it. Get the fuck outta here." He motioned wildly at the road. "I don't want fairies sucking each other's cocks in my goddamn lot." He looked at Dom. He pointed. "I don't like the way you're eatin' that sucker, boy. Don't taunt me with your lasciviousness."

He mangled the final word, but that was what he meant. That was it. That was the one too many.

I gripped the blackjack and started at him.

"Royce, don't!" Dom shouted.

The attendant, surprised, raised his hands and clenched his fists. I had no time for bullshit posturing. I vented my rage. I ran at him, ducking my head. His fist clipped the back of my skull, dislocating his knuckle but doing little damage to me. I barreled into his waist. His legs tangled, and he went down hard against the pavement with me on top. His hat fell away. He didn't know whether to hit me or cover his face. He did something in between, which is as good as nothing in the few seconds of a fight. I got the sense he'd never fought anyone, not seriously, in his life. He was a blowhard. He thought he'd stomp and make us run.

I got between his arms, rendering him weak, and I hammered his face once with the blackjack. Then and there the fight left him. It went out of him like the bell by the pump. The leather slammed his mouth, splitting his lips against his teeth. Rapidly, I hit him again, hammering down with all my fury, and caught his nose. The cartilage gave. Blood shot up my forearm and cascaded down his chin. His eyes went wide with shock. He'd never had his face opened.

When I raised my hand for a third strike, one that would put him to sleep, Dominic caught my wrist. He pulled on it. I realized then that Dom was shouting, that he'd been shouting all along. He was calling my name, begging me to stop.

The attendant stayed on his back, sniveling. He gulped for air.

Dominic pulled me to a standing position. I was short of breath, my chest heaving. My hand buzzed around the rod. A rivulet of blood snaked down my wrist toward my palm.

The attendant watched me from the pavement. A mix of blood, snot, and saliva pooled around his mouth. Terrified, he believed I was going to kill him. I saw it. If Dominic hadn't been there to stop me, I can't say how far I would've taken it.

Too far, likely. I wanted to hit him again.

"You say a goddamn word about this and we'll be back. You don't want your buddies knowing a fairy kicked your ass, do you?"

He didn't say anything. He swallowed blood. He was too hurt to think straight. His tongue explored a cracked tooth. I'd broken it at the root, but it hadn't come undone. Half attached, it hung. His face turned a shade of green when he realized what his tongue probed.

I pointed the blackjack at him like a cop with his billy club.

"You understand what I'm saying to you?" For the first

time, I read the name on the front of his coveralls. "Spencer, you understand?"

He rose onto his elbow and nodded curtly. His face was swelling. He needed a doctor, but I wasn't going to call one for him. He knew where the telephone was located.

Dom yanked my arm. He watched the highway, as if cops would swoop in. We were in the middle of nowhere, though.

"Let's go," he said tightly.

I shrugged him off. Then, feeling like a weight had been lifted, I turned my back on the attendant. I walked around the front of the Cadillac and opened the door. Dom was already inside. I handed him the blackjack. I pulled a hand-kerchief from my pocket and wiped sweat from my face. Then I handed the rag to Dom to clean the blood off the leather.

The attendant stood and started back to his shack. His chin dripped blood. No other cars were in sight.

When I was inside with the ignition turned, I looked at Dom. I didn't share his shame, and I didn't share his shock. I didn't feel much of anything other than relieved. I pulled the car onto the highway.

After we'd gone a few miles in silence, he rolled up his window to quiet the noise and said, "What the hell was that? I've never seen you like that, Royce."

I answered the question with another. "Where'd your sucker go?"

"In the dirt back there."

"Wanna go back and get another one?" I side-eyed him and laughed.

He'd been holding the blackjack this entire time, I realized. He finally placed it in the glove box.

"Where'd you learn to do that?" Dominic asked.

"Too many movies," I said.

He didn't share the joke. Rather, his face became a mask of dismay.

"Light a cigarette for me," I said.

"You going to tell them to call you Mr. Tibbs next time?" Dom asked. He fished out a cigarette. "Like Sidney Poitier."

"I knew what you meant."

Finally, he smiled. "You broke his tooth."

"He won't talk to my man that way again, will he?"

"How many times have you done that before?" Dominic asked.

I reminded him of my time in Mansfield, and that's where the conversation died. We drove in silence.

CHAPTER TEN

The drive became scenic when we passed through the Fort Apache Reservation and entered the foothills of the White Mountains. The highway climbed ridges lined with columns of juniper and groves of velvet ash. It was beautiful country and a stark contrast to the expanses of desert that preceded it. The car scaled and descended crooked roads, while an 8-track of Claude Debussy played softly. We chose a detour to get close enough to see the snow-draped peaks, rising higher and higher through a haze off the passenger's side of the highway. The beauty of the mountains had a calming, mesmerizing effect. I watched the road less and the mountains more. Dom and I needed the distraction.

We stopped for lunch at a diner where the peaks formed a backdrop, and I took time in the restroom to change shirts and clean up. I scrubbed my hands and face, combed my hair into place, and scratched flakes of blood from my watch. I didn't feel good or bad about what had happened. I only hoped the attendant didn't call the highway patrol. That worry remained on my mind.

Dom didn't ask any more questions about my proficiency with the blackjack. For the time being, he let the subject go, although we both knew it would resurface. He was too bothered by the display for it not to arise. Dominic wasn't naïve, and I don't want to paint him that way. He'd seen brutality at the bars he played, but he'd never witnessed something like that from me. I couldn't tell whether he liked the proclivity, loathed it, or found it frightening. He would have to let the matter settle. Then he'd know. He'd decide.

While we picked at plates of greasy meatloaf, Dom moved on to talking about Spaghetti Westerns and Clint Eastwood, and how Italy and Spain looked nothing like Arizona. It was empty rambling, just chatter. He then talked about Vietnam and a holiday called Tet. I picked at the terrible food and listened. Hearing his voice was a comfort. I didn't care what he talked about. He moved on to the curiosity of Vincent Price selling fine art through Sears Roebuck department stores. The image of a gentleman like Price hawking oil paintings in a fluorescent showroom at Sears got me laughing.

"I'm serious," Dominic said. He picked at the meatloaf I couldn't eat.

"Uh-huh." I slid the plate toward him.

"He does commercials for it!"

"Uh-huh."

We drove on, and we exited the mountains where the land flattened and mesquite replaced juniper. As we entered the town of Snowflake, I was fresh and respectable, poised and calm. Dom had switched 8-tracks, and now Ennio Morricone played loudly. With the windows down, it made our arrival triumphant. I wore a jacket and tie, this set ordered from Los Angeles rather than London. I looked like the doctor Saint Paul believed me to be. Dom, whom I'd presented as my assistant, stayed with the dreadful Hawaiian shirt. He was, at least, wearing his beautiful array of rings, and his 4711 cologne was enticing.

Snowflake was a small town with rows of houses along quiet streets. Stores, a few restaurants, and a city building crowded the downtown area. The only jarring aspect of the landscape was a billboard that advertised the Church of Latter Days Saints with photos of men named Erastus Snow and William Jordan Flake. The images were sepia, and a covered wagon between the photos marked them as pioneers. Civic pride. Saint Paul's UFO cult shared space with a Mormon stronghold. I appreciated the bizarre mix.

I turned the music down as we entered Main Street. A handful of pedestrians moved along the sidewalks, and a few cars crawled through, but the town was otherwise dead.

Dom blew smoke out the window. "Not impressed," he said. He waved politely at a woman and child. "Reminds me of home."

"Hick town," I agreed. I squinted out the window, reading street signs.

Following a four-way stop, I maneuvered onto a street specified in Saint Paul's directions. The lane led to a subdivision where his commune was located.

"Why's their hideaway all the way out here?" Dom asked. "These people have nothing to hide from."

"Nothing on Earth maybe," I said. "What's the next turn?"

Dom looked at the handwritten directions. "Left at the next stop sign."

"I'll tell you what he told me."

Dominic laughed. "Okay."

"One: There's no light pollution in the desert around here."

"That's way too sensible. What's the second reason?"

"Two: Natives made the land magical."

"With what?"

"Magic. I don't know. It's as racist as it sounds."

"That's why the Mormons picked it, too. What's three?"

"Three: The airspace here is a freeway for UFOs. He says they come through nightly."

"Nightly? We'll see one then, I suppose."

Gravely, I nodded.

"Turn here," Dom said.

We approached a large swath of land, enclosed by fences of piled stone. The place had been a horse farm or ranch long ago, but it was nothing of the sort today. The barn closest to the road was rotten. A section of the roof was caved. A tall knoll, covered in a switchgrass with fiery red tips, stood at the rear of the lot. I knew from Saint Paul's lectures that the knoll was a special place of contact. That's where the members communed. Nestled below the hill were several buildings, with the centermost being a sprawling ranch house. Unlike the barn, the house was kept up.

"How the hell do they afford this?" Dom asked.

"They got a trust fund kid in their ranks," I said.

I pulled up to the front entrance. Although no gate barred the drive, there was a wooden arbor with a man sitting on a stool at its corner. A tall box-elder maple gave the man shade. A bucket stood at the foot of his stool, and a stack of star maps, the type Saint Paul sold at his lectures, waited near his hand.

"It's Hoss Cartwright," Dominic whispered.

"Shut up."

"Looks like him."

Unfortunately, that was true.

Dominic lit another cigarette. "It's the fuckin' Ponderosa," he said, laughing.

I rolled to a stop before crossing the arbor's threshold. I looked at the man on the stool, and he looked at me. He was a mountain with thick shoulders and a bull neck. He was balding, and he had a gap in his teeth. The only thing missing was the ten-gallon hat. He even wore a suede vest, although his ended in long strands of fringe and covered a shirt with billowing sleeves.

Before I opened my mouth, he said, "Dr. Madigan?"

"Yes," I said. "Hello. I'm here to meet with Saint Paul." I smiled. "I assume this is the correct place."

The man nodded, and he returned the smile. "Drive on up," he said. "Oh, and Dr. Madigan?" The dreamy look that came into his eyes was unsettling. There was a disconnect between his gaze and brain—the type of damage you see from people who've taken too many psychedelics.

"Yes?" I asked, waiting.

He shook his head, smiling widely. "You won't believe what happened last night. It's better if he tells you."

"Thanks," I said.

We rolled through the arbor. "Light a cigarette for me," I told Dominic.

Searching for my pack, he said, "Fuck's sake, what have you gotten us into?"

"Maybe you can write a song about it."

He handed me the cigarette, and then he started singing "Mr. Spaceman" by The Byrds.

CHAPTER ELEVEN

The driveway ended in a gravel lot that held several old cars and a truck. All the vehicles were rusted, outdated jalopies. A twenty-year-old truck sat lopsided on three wheels. I parked the Cadillac away from the others and killed the motor. Before the car settled, a woman and man materialized. They stood at our trunk, trying to pry it open with nothing but their fingers.

"We're being attacked," Dom said. He locked his door.

I peered in the rearview and caught the man's face. Not surprisingly, he had the gaunt features of a junkie. His eyes were gone inside of his head, like the pupil was on the wrong side. The woman matched him. She looked like a vampire full of moldy bones. The couple kept at my trunk, trying to unlock it with brute strength. Their veined faces grew red with the strain. As Dom and I waited for this to pass, the car trembled on its shocks.

"Auspicious beginnings," I said, sinking low. It was difficult not to be demoralized.

Another woman came running to rescue us, shooing away the couple at our trunk. She snapped off a few wicked lines in Spanish. Her tone had bite. The junkie and his companion obeyed, releasing the trunk in turn. Slump-shouldered and chastised, they moped toward the house.

I watched our savior through the glass.

"That's enough for me," Dominic said. "I vote we turn around."

"Stop it." I put the keys in my pocket.

"Those were zombies, Royce."

"Maybe," I said.

The woman smiled at me.

"Nothing wicked about her," I said. "Look at that grin."

"Fuck this place," Dom said.

Dressed in the hippy garb that Saint Paul preferred, she placed her hands on her hips and waited. She was as short as a child, no more than five feet. She wore her hair teased and frizzed, presenting like a shocked bird. Large round glasses covered a third of her face. She wore a tank top with no bra underneath. Her pants were chaps, crocheted, held aloft by a flowered belt.

Looking at her, I was homesick. I wanted to be in the Duprey penthouse or Aguirre mansion where I belonged. Not slumming. I was above jobs like this. I missed Ardella, too.

Suck it up, I thought. *You're here. The money's too good.*

With the Lotte Holden fallout, I needed funds sorely. I took a breath and put on a face.

"Stiff upper lip," I told Dom. I patted his knee.

I crushed what remained of my cigarette and then opened the door. Reluctantly, Dominic followed my lead.

"Dr. Madigan," the woman said, looking up at me. She had a Mexican accent, although it wasn't prominent.

I shook her hand. "Yes, and this is my assistant, Dominic."

The woman looked across the car and nodded. She released my hand. A glow came over her.

"Who might you be?" I asked. I tried to make it light. "I believe you saved us."

"Luna." She wasn't particularly interested in me anymore. She watched Dominic. "Are you Italian?" she asked.

"What?" he said, caught off guard.

"Your tan. It's so even and beautiful. Wanna go lay in the sun with me?"

"Maybe some other time," Dominic said. Awkwardly, he scratched the back of his scalp. After removing his glasses, he looked around at the grounds of the commune bathed in sunlight. He lit a cigarette.

"I love Italian men," Luna told me. She bit her lip.

I smiled at Dom. At least she was his problem rather than mine. Then, to Luna, I asked, "Who were those people?" I pointed at the junkies. They stood on the front porch, hugging columns, watching us. I didn't like them. I didn't want them near me, watching me.

"They're part of the *help*," Luna said. "Saint Paul found them."

"Found them where?"

Dominic laughed.

Luna smiled at his laughter. "Anywhere," she said. "The streets. Drifters. He brings 'em in all the time. They do work for us."

Christ, I thought. *The cult has slaves*.

Saint Paul never mentioned that aspect in his recruitment lectures. He was in the wrong part of the nation for that to be a selling point, I supposed.

"It's the way you slick your hair back," Luna said to Dom. "So much grease." She giggled. "It's very Italian. I love it."

"He's not Italian," I said impatiently. "He's from West Virginia. Now, is Saint Paul around?"

"He's communing."

"Do you have a telephone I can use?"

Luna smiled. She nodded. It was a big nod with all that hair. "You can't reach him by phone," she cautioned. "That's not how he communes."

"Can you take me to it, regardless?"

She pointed at the ranch house. Several people stood on the front porch, watching. I had a tape recorder and a few other valuables in the trunk, so I wasn't keen on leaving the car unguarded. Addicts sniffed out electronics like hounds.

"Fine," I said. "Thank you. Dom, why don't you entertain Miss Luna? And stay near the car, please."

He took a drag. "What?"

I turned, putting my forearm on top of the car. I made an emphatic face at him.

He sighed and blew smoke out his nose. "Wanna trade cigarettes?" Dom asked Luna. He held up the burning clove, pinched between his fingers. "I bet what you got is better than what I got."

"Oh, I can guarantee that," Luna said.

"Tell her about that time we went to Florence," I suggested.

Dominic glared at me. "Yeah, tales of the home country," he said tightly.

"There you go."

"Your eyes are far out," Luna said. "So dark." She moved to the front of the car. She was barefoot and moving lithely, undeterred by the gravel.

Despite Dominic's pleading stare, I went to the porch. "Yeah, he's groovy," I said. "Just look at that wild shirt."

"I dig it," she said.

By the time I reached the steps, six people crowded the landing.

"Do you have a telephone I can use?" I asked no one in particular. I looked up at them from the ground. All of them looked at me. The sun beat over my shoulder.

A young, shirtless man with Beatles hair motioned for me to come inside. I followed him into a front room paneled with fake wood. It was painfully tacky. The windows were open and a couple fans were going. Sheer curtains, soiled with a colorful array of stains, billowed. The room was hot. There was so much cat piss that it made the air humid. Doodles and phrases covered the walls in a variety of hands. The telephone was mounted beside the drawing of a man gripping the bars of a jail cell. A bunch of squiggly lines came from his head to reveal his consternation. There was a message in that drawing, I supposed, a lunatic message. I thanked the young man. Then, through the operator, I put in a call to Theda Eklund in the city. I loosened my tie while I waited.

The vamp answered on the fourth ring.

"How's Ardella?" I asked.

I watched the front door as I spoke. The junkies were there, holding the frame, watching me. The others on the porch had gone.

Theda spoke over a loud television. Mixed with the cats, the noise was like a party behind her.

"She's hiding under the bed, dear, but she's fine. She didn't eat." Theda held up the mouthpiece to the room, which was unnecessary. "Can you hear them?" she asked, her voice distant.

Uncomfortably, I watched the junkies. A feline yowl caught my ear.

"He sounds mad," I said.

"Royce, they're quite bothered, and it has nothing to do with sweet Ardella. I'm glad you called." Theda went on, bringing the phone nearer. Her tone changed, grew severe, very unlike the vamp I knew. "Something…. Well, dear, something quite odd occurred this morning." She cupped the mouthpiece, quieting the cats.

An "odd" occurrence could be any number of things with Theda, from The Beach Boys on *Ed Sullivan* to an old film she watched on television, but I had an idea of where this was going. Maybe it was paranoia, but I sensed blame in her manner. My life was bleeding into her life, just as it was bleeding on the Dupreys. I was creating problems. That made me decidedly less valuable to them. The tone sank my heart.

"Go on," I said.

"Your young woman visited this morning."

In a swell of anger, I asked, "She came to your apartment?"

"Dear, it was the same woman who accosted you at the séance. Somehow, she got inside the building. She came right up to my door. She didn't try other doors. She came directly to mine."

"You didn't let her inside, did you?"

"Of course not. No. She knocked incessantly. She knocked until one of my neighbors threatened her with the police. She was nasty to him, and then she left after that. At least I assume she left. I'm slightly wary of going out, Royce, dear. She isn't in the hall at any rate. I checked."

"Christ," I said. I tried to be level.

The intrusion spoke one truth to me, however. If I ran from Anna, as I was doing now, she'd harass the people in my life until I returned. She didn't have the means to come after me, but she had the means to force my hand. I ran the cord through my fingers, feeling helpless. Being distant caused me more anxiety than being near.

"Royce, there's only one way I can imagine she found my home. She must've followed you here when you dropped off Ardella. I don't mean to alarm you, dear, but that implies she knows where you live. She's following you."

I grasped for platitudes. "I'm so sorry, Theda. I'm truly sorry she's involved you."

"She's also been telephoning Addy."

I sensed another thread in her voice. Theda, like the Dupreys, had come to rely on me for comfort. Behind her words, she was pleading with me to fix the problem, to eliminate the stress of it from her life. Just as I fixed her emotional problems, she wanted me to fix a physical problem. She was not the type of person who cared about means—she wanted problems corrected, and that was all. If she had alcohol in her she would ask me to solve the problem directly. Since it was better left unspoken, I was glad for her sobriety.

"Be safe, Royce," Theda said. "Please watch out for yourself."

"I'll make this up to you," I said. "Hold on." Cupping the phone, I asked the junkies the number for the ranch. The young man who'd escorted me inside had gone.

"Pineapple," the woman offered.

"Shirt," added the man.

"Thanks." I uncovered the phone. "Look, I'll call and check in. I'll get you a number to reach me. Eventually. Stay safe, Theda. Do not engage Anna. Call the police next time. Please call them. Tell Addy to call them. Whatever you do, don't engage her. Don't listen to her. Please."

"This is causing me a lot of anxiety, dear. I don't know what to do."

"Give me a little time," I said. "I'll take care of it."

Theda's voice lifted. "You will, dear? You promise?"

"I promise," I said. "I just need a little time."

Theda was silent.

"Tell Ardella I love her. Goodbye, Theda."

"Ciao, Royce, darling."

I placed the telephone on the hook. My mind blurred.

You have to do something about Anna, I thought. *You have to do something. You can't run.*

Do what? I knew one choice that was quite effective. *But how to do it? How to get away with it?*

I walked outside, splitting the junkies. They let me go, but they came back to the columns to watch me. Thankfully, Dom was still near the car. Luna sat on the hood, her chin on her fist. Dom was ranting about Vietnam. He had a fat joint in his hand. Luna watched him like he was a guru. I had the feeling Dominic would enjoy his stay.

How to do it? How to do it without Dominic knowing?

"Is Saint Paul finished *communing*?" I called to anyone listening. "Can somebody take me to see Saint Paul? I drove a long way to be here."

"The doctor seems angry," I heard Luna tell Dom.

"He's a very serious man," Dom said. "Dedicated to his craft."

CHAPTER TWELVE

Saint Paul's inner sanctum, his holy of holies, was an apartment above a garage. Detached, it stood at the east end of the ranch house. While his adherents crowded the house, and the junkies slept in the rotted barn, Saint Paul lived alone, a perk of being the leader.

He maintained a steady stream of visitors, however, so his existence wasn't solitary. The only time he lived the life of a hermit was during communion. From his lectures, I understood this to mean he dropped acid and opened a portal to speak with extraterrestrials. As this exchange unfolded, two women stood guard outside his door in case he did something drastic like stab himself with a letter opener.

Maybe communion also meant he was napping, because he seemed quite groggy when I entered the holy space. I thanked the woman who allowed me inside. She greeted that with a smile. She closed the door, leaving us alone.

Saint Paul lay on a divan, his leg dangling over the side. A fan moved his long hair. He wore a Persian kaftan of burgundy and gold. The embroidered robe reached to his ankles. He was nude beneath the garment. Splayed as he was, I couldn't help but notice.

From his back, he said, "Doc Madigan. How goes it, my brother?"

I recalled that he didn't smoke, so I refrained from pulling a cigarette. My nerves wanted it. Tensely, I thought about it.

"I'm impressed," I said. Impressed about what I didn't say, and he didn't ask, so I let it hang there.

I looked around the room, as if in admiration. There was no consistency to the décor. Rather, the themes of his design erupted in piles. Here there were blackout curtains stitched with crescent moons, faces, and colorful symbols. There was a tapestry with the words *Love Thy Neighbor* sewn in a shaky hand. Beads hung everywhere beads could hang. Burned spoons, lighters, matches, and candle stubs were mixed with stacks of books and tufts of pamphlets. A map of stars covered one wall, framed by graffitied Polaroids of the night sky. The face of an alien with whom Saint Paul communed covered another wall. It was a large face with enormous eyes and a tapered chin. A table with an array of candles and owl figurines stood beneath the portrait. Incense burned there. A telescope stood beside the shrine.

Near the curtains was an austere wooden desk with a typewriter. An overflowing manuscript box waited beside the machine. Saint Paul was, I understood, writing a mystical memoir. That was one reason he wanted me to work with him. He wanted to tease out details for his book.

I'd do that. I had a lot of ideas ready.

Saint Paul rose on his elbow. With his free hand, the bizarre man executed a mudra. Then he lifted a pamphlet from a coffee table in front of the divan. He flung it my way. The literature dropped at my shoes. I picked it up and read the cover. It was for an organization based out of Tucson called the APRO (Aerial Phenomena Research Organization).

"What do you know about them?" he asked pointedly.

Thankfully, I'd never claimed expertise on UFOs. I didn't have to make anything up, so I shrugged. "I'm afraid I'm unfamiliar."

"Take a look," Saint Paul said. He swung his legs over and sat straight. He channeled another mudra. He picked up dark-lensed glasses and hid his eyes behind them.

I stepped to the window where sunlight fell across the floor. I scanned the document until I got the gist. The APRO claimed a scientific approach to investigating UFOs, with believers and skeptics composing their ranks. Such composition balanced their approach. It was the usual obnoxious attempt to turn a fringe, inherently unbelievable field mainstream. Spirit mediums had the Parapsychology Lab at Duke University. UFOnauts had the APRO. It was belief in search of respect—a wrongheaded notion.

Saint Paul shared my assessment of the APRO. "Claptrap," he said. "We keep receiving those in the mail."

I turned to him. "For what purpose?"

Saint Paul did a mudra. "They don't like me, man. They don't dig what we're doin' out here. They're tryin' to convert us like the Mormons try to convert us. We are on a hill with invading armies around us. You're holdin' a piece of artillery, a spent shell."

I flipped the pamphlet to the back cover. "I saw the Mormon billboard," I said absently.

Saint Paul grew serious. "We're gonna put one up right beside it." He pointed at the face on the wall. "She's gonna be on it. Sister-fuckin' Mormons and their magic underwear, man. They don't stop. They don't take hints."

A list of names ran down the back of the pamphlet: important persons in the organization. Amid the PhDs, one of the names gave me a start. Ignoring Saint Paul, who had more to say about Mormons, I read the list again. I wasn't mistaken. Karl Landrum was a member of the APRO, and he was prominent enough to be featured on the brochure. A PhD followed his name—a detail he'd omitted from the Dupreys. A touch of claustrophobia moved me, a sense of the cage door banging shut.

I interrupted the sage—something to which he was unaccustomed, especially in his holy of holies. I approached with the pamphlet. I pointed at the name.

"This man here, do you know him? Karl Landrum?"

"I thought you didn't know anything about them," Saint Paul said. He scratched the wiry hair on his chin.

I watched my reflection in his glasses. "I know him."

Saint Paul slipped on sandals and stood from the divan. I tried to be patient as he shuffled to a cabinet. I shoved the pamphlet into the pocket of my jacket. From the junk, he pulled a box of matches.

"I don't do safety matches," he said. "Everybody tryin' to protect us from everything, man. It's hard to find these, brother." He held up the box for my inspection. They were "strike anywhere" matches, and the box was old. By his manner, I assumed he had a point with the contrivance, so I indulged his "teaching."

Saint Paul freed a match. Aided by a flick of the tongue, he lit the match on his teeth. Fire erupted near his lips. He put the flame to a stick of incense then shook it dead. A tendril of smoke roiled into the air.

"They don't want kids doin' that, man. Understand? They don't want you buyin' these because *they* wanna protect you. You can't find 'em because *they* think they know better. Like a lot of things, they hide 'em." He struck another match on his teeth. He let the stick burn to his fingers before extinguishing it. "You ever do that as a kid?"

No, I thought. *I'm sane.*

I moved a stack of magazines from a chair and sat. "I assume you know Landrum," I said.

"He's a straight-up prick, Doc. He's one of those that thinks he knows better than everybody. He's full of warnings. He'd gasp about 'strike anywhere' matches. He'd lecture me. You know what I mean, man?" Saint Paul lit another match on his bare knee. The odor drifted across the room.

"How do you know him?"

"He's the fucker that mails all that shit, man."

"How do you know he mails it?"

"He told me."

I rubbed my forehead. The room felt too close. I tried to relax, but the incense and brimstone got inside my head.

"Man, what about all that gets you uptight? You need a drink, brother?"

"What do you have?"

"Homemade wine. World-class exquisite, man. How 'bout it?"

I declined. "Will you please have a seat?" I asked.

"Sure," Saint Paul said. He sat on the divan with—*goddamn him*—his knees spread. He lit a match on the coffee table.

I crossed my legs and reclined. "Did Landrum have anything to say about me?" I asked in a measured tone.

Saint Paul smiled. It was a palsied smile that occupied only one corner of his mouth.

"He did, man. He said you're a fake." He let that settle.

I took it in stride. I knew where this was going, so there was no shock in it.

"He said what you do is nothin' more than carnival tricks, except there's no prize at the end."

I nodded. "When did he tell you this?"

"New Year's Day, man. Right after we talked. And I mean right after." Saint Paul watched me closely. "I figured that'd make you blow your top, Doc. He's followin' you around. Why ain't it got you livid?"

"Because what he says is untrue. That man has done nothing but harass me. He's done nothing but undermine my clients' trust. I've already blown my top. The more important question is: do you believe him?"

"I said he was a straight-up prick, didn't I? Hell no, man. He thinks we're all shovelin' bullshit. Gullible, he said." He pointed at the alien face. "He thinks she's bull, too, Doc. You think I'd let you drive all the way up here to embarrass you? Shit." He shook his head. "I'm one hundred percent on your team. I know a man's character," he added.

Ironic or not, that brought relief. The relief was short lived.

"I'll tell you what I did do."

"What?" I asked warily.

"I invited him up here to see for himself, man. I'm gonna let you blow him away, Doc. Then I'll blow him away. We'll both do it. Show him he don't know shit. He can stuff those pamphlets in his asshole, man. I'll even roll 'em up and grease 'em for him."

I dug my fingers into the arm of the chair. "How'd he respond to that?"

"Oh, he's gonna be here tomorrow morning, man." Saint Paul nodded to a beat in his head. "Bringin' his wife."

"Can I smoke in here?" I asked.

Saint Paul pointed to the open window. "Yeah, but blow it out there, man. Air's pristine in here."

"Thanks." I stood and walked to the window. I got out a Chesterfield. I pinched off the filter. What Dom didn't know wouldn't hurt him.

Saint Paul lit another match with his mouth. He came over with it.

"Where else can you light them?" I asked.

"Anywhere," he said sincerely. He motioned around—at me, the room, the whole universe. "Got a request?" He pulled another match from the box.

Yeah, I had a request. I left it unsaid.

CHAPTER THIRTEEN

At dusk, Saint Paul's people kindled a large fire in the pasture beneath the knoll. There were no more buildings behind the ranch house, only an open expanse with islands of green to interrupt the sandy dirt. Men and women dragged in whatever debris they found to feed the blaze. When one of the junkies poured gasoline, the flames roared, climbing dangerously high. Like busy ants, the cultists worked at the fire for the better part of an hour. They needed something that could be seen from outer space.

Saint Paul stood atop the hillock, with a woman on each arm, coordinating the activity. With his robe fluttering at the hem, he reminded me of Moses on Mount Sinai. No doubt he thought himself of similar importance. I'd never asked why he called himself Saint Paul, but I assumed he had his own ideas about God.

Dominic and I waited in a bedroom that was cordoned off for our use. Small as it was, I appreciated the gesture. If it wasn't faux pas, we would've slept at one of the hotels in Snowflake. It was faux pas, so here we were, in a space the size of a child's room. The only light was ambient light because the fixture on the ceiling had been ripped out by the roots. Wires dangled from the cavity. Someone had taped down the switch on the wall from fear of fire. A couple twin mattresses with sun-bleached sheets lay on the floor. The beds were strikingly uninviting. I sensed the needles and lice in their folds. I wanted nothing to do with them. We needed a peasant to roll on them to ascertain their safety before we partook.

Aside from the mattresses, a single window looked out upon the pasture and bonfire. In one corner of the room there was a pile of old clothes, rags, and garbage swept hastily off the floor. Two creaky wooden chairs stood by the window. The walls were wood paneling covered in drawings and phrases. The entire house was like that. Even the ceiling was marked with signatures. Unpleasantly, it reminded me of incarceration at Mansfield.

Dom snorted two more lines from the back of his acoustic guitar. When he finished, he shook his head and smacked at his nose. Playfully, he smiled at me and shuddered like a wet dog. He washed the cocaine down with a drink of beer. The cocktail he'd ingested over the day had him wired. He had no blood in his face or hands—all the blood worked on his heart.

"Is being in a cult a crime?" he asked.

I hadn't told him about Karl Landrum because I had an idea brewing. I wanted Dominic to have fun tonight. I wanted him out of my hair, incapacitated. I watched him, smoked, and was pensive. I snapped off the filter without him noticing. I flicked ash out the window. A can of Blatz stood on the sill, sweating, untouched. Wood smoke entered the room.

"Wait until you're abducted before you ask for an application," I said.

He licked the residue from his guitar and flipped it over. He reclined, mashing a few chords, strumming. He played snippets from the ballad in *Django*. He'd been working up Spaghetti Western music for his folk sets. He liked the idea of mixing bombastic sounds with lyrics about the Battle of Khe Sahn. I thought the idea stunk.

I crossed my legs, watching the window. The sky darkened. The fire grew stronger, deeper, taller.

Dom stopped humming and asked, "No word on Anna?"

"Nothing."

"You called?"

"I'll call again. I believe she's going to burn out," I said. "It isn't getting her anywhere."

He strummed another chord. The room was cool. The night was cool.

"Why do you say that?" He squinted his eyes, trying to focus. He was too far gone for concentrating, but his appetite remained large. I knew Dominic wasn't finished. He planned to drop acid on the knoll with Saint Paul. I'd encouraged him to do so as my surrogate.

He's got a level head, I'd told the mystic.

"Just a feeling," I said. "Maybe a little optimism."

When he finished the beer, I handed him my can. He measured it in his hand.

"You didn't touch it," he said. "You ought to cut loose tonight, Royce. You need to blow some steam." Then he went there again. The feeling was there—that's all. "Especially after this morning."

"Have to keep a professional air. He thinks I'm a doctor," I added. "I have to be uptight. Aloof."

In truth, I had another reason for maintaining my sobriety. There were a few variables left to align, but the idea snowballed.

"Well, you look it," Dom said. He laughed. "At least take off your tie, man."

I loosened the tie some more, but it stayed on.

"Dom, how do you really feel about what happened this morning? What I did to that man at the gas station."

"It was a one-off thing. I don't know."

"You brought it up, so you must feel something about it."

He shrugged.

"What if I said it wasn't a one-off thing? What if—"

He squinted. He gulped another drink of beer. He was on the ground, and I was in the chair. With the cold look on my face, Dom thought I was bullying him.

"You're killin' my buzz," he said. "I don't wanna think about it."

That's why you're staying here tonight, I thought. *I have ideas about you, and you have ideas about me. I don't want to disturb those things.*

Silence passed between us. More smoke wafted into the room. It was too harsh. I closed the window.

Finally, Dom asked, "Was it a one-off thing or wasn't it, Royce?"

I uncrossed my legs and leaned forward. "Come here," I said.

He put his guitar and beer on the ground and crawled over. I touched his chin and kissed him. He tasted like he smelled.

"It was a one-off thing," I said. "I promise."

"I didn't like it," Dom whispered. "It wasn't you, Royce."

I kissed him. I touched his hair.

"It wasn't me. It won't happen again. I won't let myself get carried away like that anymore. I was angry is all. Everything built up." I looked in his eyes. "You know I'm not like that. It was just everything building up."

Dom sat on his ass, out of my reach. "Sometimes I just wanna be normal," he said. He grimaced at the slip of tongue.

"Normal? What's normal, Dom?"

Maddeningly, he shrugged again.

"We live well," I countered. "We're only going to live better. We're never going to live badly. This," I said, pointing at the bed, "is a one-off thing, too."

"That's not what I mean." Dominic stared at the floor.

"That's the only normal I understand," I said. I thought Dom understood that, too. "Living like we deserve to live." Defensively, I almost reminded him of the china I'd bought him, or the jewelry, or the holidays in Europe. I stopped myself on the precipice of Florence.

"Sometimes I think that's what separates us," he said.

With the rest of my life teetering, that jarred me. I didn't like it.

"What do you mean?"

"I don't know."

My anger swelled, but I kept it in check. I clenched my teeth.

"What do you mean, Dom?"

He stretched out on the floor. "I'm too rattled to think," he said. His face was pale.

For the first time in our twelve years together, the thought of hurting Dominic entered my mind. We'd had our fights, but I'd never felt the resentment and anger he inspired in that moment. Perhaps it was situational. I didn't discount that. I didn't want the image to enter my mind, yet it did. It went as quickly as it came, a flash that left me ashamed. I saw Dominic on the floor, his head opened. The image was in black and white like I'd captured it from the news. I blamed the transgression on stress, but I knew better. I knew myself. I knew what I was capable of doing.

Don't say anymore. Internally, I begged him. *Just stop. Don't make me angrier, Dominic. Don't dash what I've built here. Don't dash my image of you.*

We stayed silent until a knock at the door chased tension from the room. Dominic sat up straight. I stood and walked to the flimsy door. I opened it. There was no lock, no chain.

Luna was in the hallway. Nothing had come along to dampen her smile. She looked around me at Dominic.

"I was hoping you'd bring out your guitar," she said. "Come out. We're waiting for you."

"Go ahead," I told Dom. I looked at Luna. "Mind if I use your telephone first?"

"No, Doc, that's fine. I believe you know where it's at by now." She smirked.

I thanked her. As I started toward the telephone, Dominic stood shakily.

"Are you okay?" Luna asked. She walked over to help him.

"I just need to find my second wind," Dom said.

CHAPTER FOURTEEN

To the operator's chagrin, I declined the answering service twice. As a television set droned over my shoulder in the front room, I insisted on putting through a third call. This time someone answered. It was a man rather than Addy or Florinda. I didn't recognize his voice, but there was nothing inviting about his tone. I turned, resting my back against the wall, watching the black-and-white light of the television in the dark room.

Cautiously, I said, "Hello. I'd like to speak with Addy."

The man was terse. "She isn't available," he said.

A tick of silence passed.

"I'd like to speak to Florinda then."

"Likewise, she isn't available."

More silence came between us.

"When will either be available?" I asked.

"They won't be available."

"How about tomorrow?"

"Listen, I don't want you calling here anymore. I don't want you to have anything to do with my sisters. Do you understand, sir?"

My sisters. Ian Duprey.

"Do I know you?" I asked.

"Thankfully, you do not. I'm not gullible enough to know you. My name is Ian Duprey, and I am a brother of Adelaide and Florinda. I know who you are, so do not bother introducing yourself. I no longer want you speaking to them."

I took the openhanded smack with grace. "May I ask why?"

"Sir, you are a bloodsucking worm. That's why. You are a predator, and I have had absolutely enough of you and your ilk playing mind games with my sisters. You are a *Svengali*, and you deserve to be imprisoned for making prey of such delicate, vulnerable women. They are widowed, elderly, and lonely. You disgust me. You harm them. Is that reason enough, sir?"

It felt as though a sinkhole opened beneath me. Everything I cherished was tumbling into that hole, while Anna stood down in the pit, waiting for me to join her, watching with glee.

"Can't they speak for themselves?" I asked.

"Not anymore. No."

I broke character, and the real Royce Pembrook, the one who was acquainted with the gutter, appeared. Although my voice was level, I was seething.

"She got to you, didn't she?"

"Don't get esoteric with me. I have no idea of whom you speak, sir."

"Anna Vogel," I said softly, absently.

Ian Duprey geared up for another rant, but I stopped him by placing the telephone on the hook. A red curtain clouded my mind, so I stood breathing in the dark, staring into the glow of the television set.

I knew one thing for certain: Ian was able to stop his sisters' outgoing checks. The Duprey women were not completely free in managing their fortune, as Florinda had confided. Their brother had power of attorney. He was therefore able to grind me under his heel.

Svengali, I thought, raging.

I took out my wallet. I removed the sliver of paper that the cop holding Anna gave me. I lifted the telephone and put through another call on Saint Paul's dime.

An attendant at a homeless shelter answered on the first ring.

My desires wound tighter, coalescing, speaking with one another, agreeing.

"Is there an Anna Vogel among your wards?" I asked.

In a bored tone, he said, "One moment, sir." The shuffling of papers traveled over the line.

I was getting sore with the "sirs." I didn't want to hear another one. I waited, watching the television screen some more. It was footage of a helicopter racing over the jungle.

"She is, sir. Ms. Vogel checked in again tonight."

"Is it possible to speak with her?"

"I'm afraid not, sir. We don't encourage that."

"What's your address?"

He told me. It was in the city. I had a vague idea of where.

"Would you like me to deliver a message?" he asked.

"Tell Anna I'll be there to pick her up tonight. About four hours from now."

"Can I have your name, sir?"

"No," I said. I hung up.

First the Holdens. Now the Dupreys. I wouldn't hold on to Theda long if I lost Addy and Florinda. She'd follow their lead. I took out a cigarette and lit it. The smoke calmed me.

You can still salvage it, I thought. *You have too much history with Addy and Florinda to be cast aside easily. Their brother is only a barrier. He's only a roadblock. He can't guard them forever. He won't try. He's an important man. He's busy.*

You can salvage your life.

The life I deserve, I thought.

Emotions swelled, mixed, vomited. I breathed heavily around the Chesterfield. My chest heaved with panic. My foot tapped. I leaned on the wall and closed my eyes. I drew inward.

You can salvage your life, but you know what you must do.

I don't want to do that, I thought. *What if I get caught? I can't go back to prison. I can't leave what I've built. I can't.*

The thought of Dominic out here while I was in there, the thought of him pursuing a "normal" life, leaving me behind, leaving me to rot, was too much to bear. It had me insane.

You have to do it. What other way is there?

She's a cancer. She'll keep spreading.

You have to do it.

What if I get caught? What then?

Don't get caught. You've never been caught before.

A screen door at the back of the house opened with a creak and then slammed shut. Footsteps followed. Dominic stood in the television's light. He watched me silently.

I breathed. I uncrossed my arms and pulled the cigarette from my mouth. I breathed until the only remnant of my panic was a tremble in my hands. I couldn't stop that, so I flicked away the cigarette, mashed it, and stuffed my hands in the pocket of my jacket. I smiled at Dominic.

"Did you call Addy?" Dominic asked.

The mask slid into place. "Sure did. She wouldn't stop going on about Thib. She has him doing a new trick." I laughed. "I'm sure she'll show it to us."

"What about Anna?"

"She stopped calling. They haven't heard from her. Thank God Addy's getting over her depression. She's out of her room now. She sounded chipper."

Dominic looked at the ground. "I wanted to apologize about what I said in there." He came forward and hugged me. "I love our life," he said, his words blurred by my shoulder. "I don't want it to change."

"It's not going to," I said. "Except for the better. We're going to keep moving up, Dom." Despite my shaky hands, I embraced him. My mind was elsewhere. I didn't feel anything except rage.

"Come outside," Dominic said.

I followed him through the hallway to the back door.

"What's Paul on about?" I asked.

"It's wild," Dominic said. "Telling us what to expect. He wants you out there to hear it. He told me to come get you." He laughed. He stopped at the screen door. "That really cheers me up about Addy. I know how much that worried you. I told you she adores you."

I smiled. "I guess she does, doesn't she? I want you to have fun tonight. When was the last time you had a good trip?"

We went out the door into the cool air. The fire burned strong and high. Smoke blended with the black sky.

"It's been a few months," Dom said.

I stuffed my hands in my pockets.

From the knoll, Saint Paul shouted, "The sky's busy tonight, boys!"

"I bet we just missed one," I told Dom.

"You just missed one!" Saint Paul shouted.

While Dominic laughed, I looked up at the stars.

CHAPTER FIFTEEN

Not all the members were invited to grace the knoll and experience the night's abduction. Most were positioned around the fire, smoking grass, bearing witness. One of the women held Dominic's guitar on her lap, plucking open strings. I was on the ground with this group, checking my watch impatiently, while Dom sat with the chosen above.

Saint Paul's circle included Dom, Luna, and four people to whom I'd only now been introduced: Trudie, Celeste, and Hazel, who protected Saint Paul, and a man in an army jacket and bandana named Abner Rood. Rood was nonverbal—that was the only thing Saint Paul said about him. Why he was selected, I didn't know, but he was set to be among the first cadre I hypnotized the following day. If he chose not to speak, it would make for an interesting time. Save for Dom, Saint Paul had selected everyone for reasons known only to him.

Of the seven (a celestial number, Saint Paul reminded me), all took a tab of acid under the tongue. After thirty minutes of watching the sky, the LSD took hold. Brain-gripped, Saint Paul ordered the circle to lie on their backs and stare upward. He had a particular star in mind. He described a constellation I didn't know about, couldn't see. He pointed with manic energy. Nobody confirmed whether they understood him or not. Collectively, the group's feet joined in a smaller circle.

It was nearing ten p.m., and I wondered if the man at the shelter gave Anna my message. I wondered what she believed about it. I wondered until my stomach was sick.

A meteorite streaked the sky, a stitch of orange on black. This sent a ripple through the crowd around the fire. One—the man who resembled Hoss Cartwright—lost his mind about the shooting star. He started speaking in gibberish. It was a nonsensical drone, but a woman near me explained that he was speaking Ancient Gaelic, which was the first language the extraterrestrials had learned from Earth, and it was the one they preferred. The aliens thought Gaelic had a musical lilt to it. English, they said, was guttural and ugly. It was a good detail, and much too much to reveal to me, so I tucked it away for the hypnosis sessions.

"Fascinating," I said. There was no real secret to my business, save for being a sponge.

The woman smiled. She put her arm around my shoulder.

"How long does this usually last?" I asked.

"All night," she said. "Until the sun rises."

"Do you ever see them lift up?"

"Their bodies stay here. It's their souls, brother. Their souls go up."

"Have you ever seen their souls go up?"

"You're Doc Madigan, aren't you?"

I nodded.

"What are you smoking?"

"Just a cigarette," I said.

She curled her nose. "I'll tell you this, brother. You ever cut your finger when it's cold? You ever see steam come out of that cut?"

"I get the idea," I said.

"That's what I saw. Soul comes out of their mouths and noses like that."

I slid free. She had atrocious body odor, and I didn't like her or anyone else here touching me. I made a show of stepping closer to the knoll so as not to offend the woman. She stepped with me.

"What's your name?" I asked.

"Sabina," she said.

"Have you ever been abducted?"

"Of course."

"Are the aliens always the same species?" I asked.

"We have contact with one civilization, but they've shown us others."

"You've met them?"

"From afar. They visit many planets. Ours is only a grain of sand in the ocean."

"That's heavy," I said. I took a long drag. I checked my watch. That was enough homework for tonight. I handed Sabina what was left of my cigarette.

She declined. "Those are terrible for your lungs," she said, disgusted.

"You know what else is bad for you?"

"What, Doc?"

I let it go. "Forget it. I need to go fetch another pack from the car." I looked at Saint Paul's circle. They were motionless as stone. I picked out Dom's hair. He breathed steadily. He had some tolerance to acid. He'd dropped enough to know how to separate his anxiety from the experience. Besides, this was safer than playing shows in a barrio dive. I figured the aliens would handle him with kid gloves, too, this being his first time on the slab.

"This will still be going on when I get back, right?"

"Don't stray far," Sabina said. "You don't want to miss the lights."

"I'll be right back," I said, "but I'll keep looking up, regardless."

Sabina reached for my arm. "Hey, I just had a premonition about you."

I looked at my watch.

"You have a kind soul," she said. "You have a wonderful aura, Doc. You're going to do remarkable things for us."

"That's kind of you to say."

"When you come back, I'll blow you."

I paused. "Uh-huh. I don't think that would be appropriate. Clinical reasons," I added.

She turned her shoulder. "A real square, though," she said.

Horror-struck by the thought, I left Sabina giggling. I walked around the house rather than drawing attention to myself with the creaky screen door. The lawn was dark and quiet. My departure didn't garner notice. With rapt engagement, Saint Paul's people watched the sky. Portentously, another shooting star had appeared.

I found the Cadillac in the gravel lot. Before getting in, I looked at the knoll behind the house once more, bathed in firelight.

Take care, Dom, I thought.

I didn't want to contemplate not seeing him anymore, but the possibility was there. It was a hobgoblin of a thought. I opened the door and climbed inside. When I turned over the engine, I left the lights off. I rolled up the gravel drive, windows down, radio down. I pulled through the front gate onto the street. There was no traffic. I buzzed with adrenaline. A trio of junkies, huddled beside the barn, watched me go. When I was free of the ranch, I switched on the beams, lighting the road.

CHAPTER SIXTEEN

———

After three numbing hours on the road, the lights of Phoenix came into view. The sharp peaks of the Sierra Estrella rose behind the city. Above the mountains, a line of purple abutted black, and then a mat of stars rolled out. The sight made me feel confident, made me feel what I was about to do was right.

The mountains beyond town got me thinking about all the things Dominic and I deserved. We deserved the big things and small things. We deserved all of it. I had no doubt of that. Dom had always wanted to go hiking in the Sierra Estrella wilderness, but I'd yet to make the trek with him. That amounted to a decade of excuses to avoid a few miles. Our current predicament, and his moping earlier, put some perspective on the desire. I owed Dominic a little normality. I could give him that. I promised myself I'd go out there with him if everything went smoothly tonight. We could even buy a Polaroid camera for the trip. I wanted more photos of us. I'd put them together in an album with the date written on the back of each.

I wondered if the Duprey dogs would enjoy a hike like that. I'd ask. If it were cool weather, I bet they would. If not cool, a Pyrenees would get too hot. The weather had to be right. Those dogs weren't out of my life, nor were their own-ers. I promised myself, too, that I'd get around Addy and Florinda's brother. Ian Duprey was nothing. Given time, his intervention would pass. Like Dom said, Addy and Florinda adored me. They were just as hurt as I was by their brother's behavior. They were worried they'd lose me, not vice versa.

Everything will be better after tonight, I promised.

I gripped the wheel, touched the gas. Signs for the city's exits passed in a blur.

What about the Landrums?

Maybe this will convince Karl to move on.

What if it doesn't?

If it doesn't, then I'll have to remove Karl and Shea, too. Nothing is going to pull me down. Nobody's going to take what I deserve.

The Cadillac hummed at seventy-five on the highway. I pushed the gas until it rose to eighty. Since leaving Snowflake, I hadn't spotted any cops along the route. I'd seen little traffic. Even now, as several roads merged into an expressway, the lanes were empty except for a few tractor-trailers. Without much thought, I swerved in and out of the truck traffic like a busy fly. It was after one a.m. With the window cracked, I listened to the whine of tires against asphalt. I ignored the bleating of a call-in program coming through static on the radio. The show lost me when a caller went on about Nixon and the upcoming election. I didn't adjust the dial when static ate the voices.

I exited the highway, rode the edge of the loop, and entered downtown Phoenix. There was something euphoric in the freedom I felt.

You're in control, I thought. *You control your life.*

My adrenaline became manic. Suddenly, the entire world

was clear in my mind. I saw the beginning, middle, and end. Not even Saint Paul could experience a better trip than that. I knew everything I needed to pilot my life (and Dom's life) to where I wanted it to go. Adversity gave me clarity. Our life was here, and it was going to stay here, and it was going to get better, not worse.

I merged behind a taxi and rolled to a stop at a traffic light. High rises lined the street, and each was a checkerboard of lights on, lights off.

I'll give Dom what he wants, and I'll get what I want, I thought, buzzing. My hands felt like they had angry insects in them. They shook all over the wheel. *I'll give the Dupreys what they want, and I'll get what I want. That's the way the world should work.*

I rolled down the window more and poked out my head. It was bizarre to the taxi driver, but I didn't care. I looked to the top of one of the skyscrapers.

I'm going to get us a penthouse on the top floor, Dom, I thought.

I watched the building admiringly until the driver behind me smashed his horn. The light was green. The taxi was a block ahead.

I reeled in my head and let off the brake.

Alright, I thought, *gather yourself. Get calm. You're drawing attention.*

I drove on. I breathed. I steadied my hands.

The homeless shelter where Anna lived was on South 12th Street, an old part of town. There was no traffic behind me, so I rolled slowly by the address, taking in the building. The shelter was an old church with a brick façade. A mission where you listened to a sermon before eating or hosing your ass. The structure was prewar, crumbling at the corners.

There was a paid lot across the way without an attendant, so I pulled in. I found an open spot near the rear. Brick buildings rose on each side, and all the windows were dark. Before calling on Anna, I removed my jacket and tie, folded each, and placed them in the trunk. I looked around the lot for anyone watching. As far as I could tell, I was alone. The night was quiet. Despite the cool air, I rolled up my sleeves to the elbow. I placed my rings and watch in the pocket of my jacket. I felt exposed without them. Quietly, I shut the trunk and locked it. I put the keys in one pocket and the blackjack in the other.

Get calm, I told myself. I took several deep breaths.

The shelter stood across the way. Except for a few parked cars, the street and sidewalks were empty. I lit a cigarette and waited at the edge of the lot. I watched up and down the road. A single traffic light in the distance shifted from green to yellow to red without any cars to heed it. All night on a timer it cycled through lights. I kept a hand in my pocket, loose over the blackjack, in case I got a surprise.

I had two worries. One, Anna wouldn't show. Two, she'd show with a companion, possibly a goon from the shelter she'd taken in as a protector. If the latter happened, I'd have to find a graceful way to back out without getting my head busted.

A squat brick wall enclosed the front of the parking lot. I moved down the barrier until I was between streetlights, and then I sat on the edge. The longer I waited, the more my nerves worsened. I went from good outcomes to bad outcomes, a swing that had me wanting to return to my car and head out. My resolve was delicate.

I put a spotlight on myself, which you don't do in those situations.

What are you doing?

I don't know. What am *I doing?*

Before that line of thinking became destructive, I caught movement to my left. I lowered my cigarette, letting it burn, and watched. My worries faded. A single figure, petite, turned the corner on the sidewalk. A lone woman walked my way.

I hopped from the wall. I moved into the nearest halo of light. I wanted Anna to know I wasn't trying to be a bandit, wasn't trying to remain unseen. I discarded the cigarette. I took my hands out of my pockets and stood vulnerable. It was an invitation.

I knew Anna. Warped by prison or not, I knew what she'd look for.

She approached, entering the light. She wore the same slacks and shirt she'd been wearing during our earlier encounters. It was the only suit of clothes she owned.

"I knew you'd fuckin' break, you asscock," she taunted, as if she were in control, as if she were orchestrating this. Warily, she gazed back and forth along the street and then at the interior of the lot.

I kept my hands free and open. I leaned into her ego.

"Okay," I said, "so you knew it. You were right, Anna. I have to give you credit. You brought me to my knees. I'm here begging."

Anna smiled like a stroke victim. She was, I realized, peppered. Bruises along her wrists and hands said it was heroin. The lack of flesh around her face and neck said the addiction had gripped her for some time. She was a husk.

I hated her deeply. I hated her failures, her poverty, her broken demeanor. She had fallen to the status of an urchin, pitiful and disgusting, and there was no pretense anymore. She didn't try to rise above her station. She preferred to pull me down instead. Nothing would give me more pleasure than seeing her dead in a gutter.

I lifted my chin. "Anna, I want to help you," I said. "Will you get in the car with me?"

"Why would I do that?" she asked. With hooded eyes, she watched me.

"You came out here, didn't you? I think you want this to break as bad as I do."

"I got nothin' but fuckin' time," she slurred.

"I want to help you," I repeated. I reached out my hand to her. She looked at it, and then she looked at me, puzzled. "It's obvious the Landrums aren't helping you very much. Why help them?"

She didn't say anything to that.

I kept my hand out. Finally, delicately, Anna took it. Her fingers were callused and cold.

"Come with me," I said.

"I got a knife," Anna told me. "Don't fuckin' try anything. I've fantasized killin' you many times."

"I won't try anything."

I led her into the lot. We walked to the Cadillac.

"What are they paying you?" I asked.

Anna snapped her hand away. "You ruined my life." Her face pinched into a scowl. "Why are you here?" she asked. She was confused, in a haze. She took the knife from her pocket. It was a switchblade, about three inches of steel with a wooden handle. She sprung it open. Shakily, she brandished the weapon.

I went for the blackjack.

"What do you want?" she asked. "Who are you?"

I stepped back. "Put it away, Anna," I said. "I'll brain you right here. You know I'll do it, too."

Anna looked at the blackjack. The sight of it brought the lopsided grin. For the moment, she returned to earth.

"Remember this?" I asked. "It's the same one I used on Wendell Marsh. Do you remember that night?"

"He's dead now," Anna said. "Newt's dead, too. Did you know that?"

"Yes," I lied. "And Ruben?"

She didn't answer. "How'd you fuckin' get away with all that?" Anna asked. She lowered the blade.

"You have to know the right people," I said. I watched the knife. "Fold it and put it away."

Anna collapsed the switchblade. She stuffed the weapon in her pocket.

"I want to know the right people," she slurred.

"I said I'm here to help you, didn't I?" I put away the black-jack. "How much are the Landrums paying you?"

"Not much. Some dope here and there."

"What if I got you back in the business? I know the people to do it."

The thought got in her head. I saw the change in her eyes.

We reached the car. I opened the passenger door. "Get in," I said.

She looked at me with odd sincerity.

"You wanna kill me, don't you? You don't wanna fuckin' help me."

"No," I said. "I want to make you an offer."

She chewed on that for a second. "A better offer?" she asked.

"Significantly better," I said. "With them, you're living here." I gestured at the shelter. "I can get you uptown again."

She got in the car. "I'd rather you fuckin' killed me," she muttered.

Goddamn pathetic, motherfucking trash, I thought, rushing around the back of the Cadillac.

CHAPTER SEVENTEEN

I rolled down the window to get Anna's stink out of the car. By the time we got back on the highway toward Snowflake, it was after two a.m. My dashboard showed a quarter tank. Tractor-trailers still dominated the road. We passed a charter bus leaving town.

"How'd you get out here?" Anna asked.

She smoked one of my cigarettes. It didn't do much to sober her, but the action kept her from falling asleep. The heroin was coming down hard, so it was a difficult fight. She was on the verge of a crash. I'd told her to curl up and get some rest, sleep if she wanted, because we had a drive ahead. She chose to fight it.

"We took a Greyhound," I said, watching signs pass. "Dom and I came out here in '56."

"No fuckin' shit? Right after everything went down?"

I nodded.

"I guess you know where I went in '56."

"Better question is how'd you get out here? You really travel all the way across the country to fuck me over?"

Anna rolled down her window. She blew smoke into the wind. Dirt lined her fingernails. Tobacco juice stained the tips. She looked rancid.

"Karl Landrum got me out here," she said. "I came out by bus like you."

I passed a couple semis and merged into the right lane. For a moment, I looked at the stars over the desert and thought about Dominic. He was, presumably, out there in space. I had hopes of meeting him when he awakened/returned. It wasn't out of the question yet.

After a moment, I asked, "Why Landrum?"

"I don't know if I should tell you all that, old boy." Anna smirked. She laughed out some smoke.

"Get off it," I said. "If you want my help, you're going to divulge all of it."

She was quiet but unbothered. She closed her eyes.

"Start talking," I said firmly.

"Royce, you can't do shit to help me. Who says I fuckin' want your help?" She slurred the last of that. She shook her head to wake up. When she forgot the cigarette, the ember burned the edge of her finger. That startled her back to life.

"You got in the car. It wasn't at gunpoint. That says enough."

"I was hopin' you'd fuckin' kill me," Anna mused. "I don't remember you bein' such a nice bastard. I pictured the fairy that offed his grandpa and let the world blame his mother. Cold, soulless piece of cocksucking garbage."

I ignored all that. "I tried to help you once before, didn't I?"

"And what'd that get you?"

"I can start you back into telling fortunes," I said. "I'll arrange a séance for you, Anna. I've got enough pull in town for that. I know people at a year-round amusement park called Legend City. They run shows."

She looked out the window at passing lights. There was a Christmas decoration on one of the light poles that a worker forgot to take down. It was a wreath with holly in it. Anna craned her neck to watch it as we passed. She searched the rearview mirror, but the wreath was gone.

She said, "Landrum started writing when I was in Moundsville." She finished the cigarette and flicked away the butt. "He sent a few letters. Gave proof of employment for my parole. Greased the wheels."

"You ever meet him in person?"

"Sure. We're intimate."

"Yeah?"

"Yeah. I sucked his fuckin' cock the other night." Anna laughed.

"He seems the type to demand favors like that."

Anna shrugged.

"Why does he have a problem with me?" I asked.

"I don't think he gives a fuckin' shit about you. He's just doin' a job. Me, I fuckin' hate you. Didn't take much to lure me out here to fuck you over. Rube's gonna die in prison, so fuck him. Fuck you."

"You're not writing your old man?" I asked.

"Haven't for a couple years. Don't care."

"You were supposed to go to Pittsburgh," I said.

"Fuck Pittsburgh. Fuck Rube. Fuck you."

"Landrum's doing a job for whom?"

Anna shook her head. "Whom," she muttered. "You pretentious fuckin' ass. No. I ain't that dumb."

"Ian Duprey?" I asked. "Did that asshole hire Landrum to discredit me? Then Landrum hired you to do the dirty work? Is that how it is?"

Anna shrugged. "You know this don't settle things between us, don't you? You already took away my life. I ain't stoppin' now that I'm out here. Fuck Landrum."

"How are you going to sit here and say that about me?"

"Easy."

"You tried to send me to jail again. And for something your old man did. So, you got fucked and I got lucky. That's how it goes. How's that me taking your life away?"

"What if I took the wheel and rammed us into one of these fuckin' trucks?" Anna said.

The whining roar of a semi reached us. I sped ahead of it.

"You think that would make the news?" she asked. "We deserve to go like that. We're miserable trash, Royce. No matter how you dress it up, you're nothin' but a fuckin' con."

"I help people," I said tightly.

"You con people. You're fake. Everything about you is fuckin' fake. The way you talk and dress. This fuckin' car. Everything you do and say is about building somethin'. I've had a lot of time to think about you. You're a fuckin' sick bastard, Royce. Sick in the head. Why do you always pick on old ladies? Tell me that, huh? That's helpin' people? Old hags with dead kids and dead husbands? Lonely old bags with cash. Fuck you. I had a lot of time to think about what we did. It ain't right. None of it is fuckin' right. I don't want nothin' to do with it anymore. No fortunes. Fuckin' none of it."

I checked my rage by lighting a cigarette. "That squares you with God then," I said. "Don't tell me you were sucking the chaplain's cock, too."

"World would be better off if I grabbed the wheel," Anna said. "News wouldn't say fuckin' shit about it, but it'd be true. The world would be one ounce better."

"What if I said to hell with the job and gave you cash to do something for me?"

Anna reclined her head, relaxing. Her fight against sleep ebbed.

"According to what it is. You gonna make me a fuckin' double agent? You greasy piece of shit." She laughed.

"What if I paid you to kill Landrum? Would you do it?"

She didn't think about it much. "Probably not," she said. She watched the window. "God, you're a sniveling bastard. You're a grade-A fuckin' weasel, Royce."

Silence passed.

"Where's that leave us?" I asked.

"I don't know. Maybe you can pay me to leave you alone. Maybe you can give me your clients, and I'll tell 'em it's all fuckin' bunk and set 'em free. I might even get to Heaven that way."

"Why'd you get in the car with me?"

Maddeningly, Anna laughed.

"I was kinda hopin' you'd fuckin' shoot me and leave me in the desert. Forgot how much of a pussy you are. Come and beg me to stop like that. Look at you. Fuck you." She looked at me sincerely. "I really do fuckin' hate you," she said. "I always did."

I blew smoke over the steering wheel. I felt her gaze against the side of my face.

"Just pay me off," Anna said finally. "Give me some cash to fuck off."

"What happens when Landrum pays you to come back?"

"We'll cross that bridge when we get there," Anna said. "Maybe we'll repeat things. Maybe we'll do this until we're fuckin' dead."

We sat in silence for a few seconds.

"I guess that's blackmail," she mused.

"Can you point out Snowflake, Arizona, on a map?" I asked.

"I think you're psychotic. I don't think you give a fuckin' shit about anybody but you."

"That's our exit up ahead," I lied. "Snowflake's about an hour outside Phoenix."

"Why you tellin' me that? Give me another cigarette."

I gestured at the pack in the console.

She took one.

I lit it for her.

"Where the hell you get that lighter?" Anna asked.

"Genevieve Blum," I said. "Remember her?"

I exited off the highway toward Apache Junction and the Superstition Mountains.

"Cuntslut," Anna said. "Is she still fuckin' hung up on you?"

"There's no snow in Snowflake," I said. "By the name, you'd probably think there was."

"Shut the fuck up about Snowflake, Royce. Why are you tellin' me this shit? Did you finally lose it?"

"That's where I'm going to drop you off," I said. "I'm going to give you cash and put you on a bus. There's a Greyhound station there. It'll get you to St. Louis. It might get you back to Cincinnati."

"According to how much cash," Anna said. "So?"

"So what?"

"So how fuckin' much?"

The road narrowed to a single-lane passage. I took the curves in stride, delicate on the brake.

"Would $500 do it?" I asked.

"It wouldn't. Fuck you."

"How about $1,500?"

"Closer." Anna thought for a second. "More like $2,500."

"Fair enough. Cash and a ticket back to the East Coast."

Anna nodded.

"You really that easy?" I asked.

Anna laughed. "No," she said. "I got a conscience."

"What else?"

"Might need you to get on your knees and beg me first. Might need you to do that in French like you used to do. I'd like that."

"It's only $2,500 if you give me one more thing."

"Now you're actin' like Landrum. I thought you were a fairy," Anna quipped. She smoked and laughed. She rested her head and closed her eyes.

"You're going to tell me who hired Landrum. I don't want any bullshit either."

She shook her head. She was about to fall asleep. "You fuckin' said it already," she slurred. "It's a man named Duprey."

"Ian Duprey."

"He's some relation to those old ladies you're fuckin' along. You oughta heard some of the shit I spewed on the phone." She opened one eye and grinned at me.

"I heard."

Anna was quiet for a moment. Her head drooped. I took the cigarette from her hand before it burned her fingers. I threw it out the window. I liked the idea of her sleeping. She looked up.

"Where's your boyfriend?" she asked.

"Believe it or not, he's up in space."

Anna didn't try to figure that one out. She nodded as if that were a reasonable answer. She looked out at the dark landscape silvered with moonlight. We were beyond street-lights. She leaned on the frame so that the wind blasted her.

"Did you ever hear about the Lost Dutchman's Mine?" I asked. "It's supposed to be out this way."

"I hate you so fuckin' much," Anna muttered.

"Supposed to be a gold mine hidden in the mountains.

People travel up here all the time looking for it. I hear some people come up here every summer and search. Year after year for their whole lives."

Anna groaned. She turned sideways in the seat, pulling up her knees.

"Some German found it a hundred years ago. Never told anyone where it was. His name was Waltz, maybe. Something like that." I snapped my fingers. "Jakob Waltz," I said.

"Uh-huh," Anna said groggily.

When we reached the North Apache Trail where the houses and buildings cease and the land's nothing but sand and bramble, I pulled to the side of the road. I didn't have time to get Anna all the way out to the mountains. It was a good idea, but I didn't want to waste the night. Morning was distant, but not very. The clock was against me.

Anna was asleep or in twilight. She let out a pint-sized snore.

Wouldn't it be a gas if she overdosed? I thought. *I'd prop her up against a cactus and let the sun mummify her. It'd be like in one of the old westerns, face dry and hard as sandpaper, blistered red. We'd see it on the news. They'd think she was a hitchhiking hippie.*

I took the key out of the ignition and stuffed it in my pocket. The headlights dimmed to nothing. I opened my door. The road was empty both ways. There was a town ahead, and mountains beyond that, but this was no-man's-land, desolate, arid country. With delicacy, I closed my door and walked around the front of the Cadillac. Gravel crunched beneath my step. The heat of the engine got in me as I passed. It felt good in the cold air. While slipping on a pair of leather gloves, I moved to the passenger door. The window was open, and Anna's head hung out of it.

Sensing my presence, she blinked awake.

"Anyway, they made a movie about it," I went on. "You know how I'm crazy about movies. You can catch them on television now. That's something that's changed since you were in. Dom and I watch old movies all the time. Do you remember how expensive televisions used to be? Everyone has one. Your shelter probably has one. Did Moundsville have one?"

I opened Anna's door and put my hand out to prop her up. She shook her head, fighting sleep. "I dozed off," she said.

"You must've had a big dose," I said. "Landrum pay for that?"

"What are you doing?"

"We're here," I said. "Let's get you a ticket and some cash."

I pulled her arm as she tried to look around.

"Where's the station?" she asked.

"The movie's an old western called *Lust for Gold*. You like that? I think it's a rather good title. Stars Glenn Ford and Ida Lupino. Terrific movie."

I pulled Anna out of the car. She looked ill. Maybe her trip really was going south. In close proximity, I smelled her essence. She had the scent of a dog's ass in summer.

"You look like you need some air. You want to walk out there with me?"

"For what? Fuckin' get off me." She jerked her arm.

"Have to get your cash."

"You got buried fuckin' treasure or somethin'?" Anna said. She pinched her eyes. She staggered.

I shut the car door.

"Have to walk it off," I said. "Can't go into Snowflake looking like that. They'll know you're high. Mormons run that town. They're uptight. They'll call Joseph Smith and the cops if you have bloodshot eyes."

Anna stopped. Terror surfaced in her gaze. She half wanted to die, but it was only half. The other side of her wanted everything. The other side of Anna was jealous, covetous, full of rage. One side wanted to stand and take it. The other side wanted to run.

I took the blackjack out of my pocket. I gripped it.

"Funny enough, that picture's also called *Bonanza*. I learned that in an issue of *Photoplay*. Of course, this was before the show *Bonanza*. We're talking ten years before."

Anna turned back to the car. One hand shot for the handle and the other went for the switchblade in her pocket. She didn't reach either.

I swung the blackjack. The bar caught the edge of her skull, hard enough to send Anna crashing against the door sideways. She gasped and struggled to her knees. She reached for the knife but came up with nothing. I reached down and grabbed the front of her shirt. The seams ripped. I pulled her nearer and struck her left ear, the blackjack connecting with a solid thud. That blow did something to her brain because she stopped fighting. She slumped, banging her forehead on the sand, as if she were sick. She breathed. Her back moved. She was in a lot of pain.

I stood over Anna. I had the blackjack cocked for another blow.

She started crying. She tried to speak, but it came out garbled. She made sounds into the sand.

"Anyway," I said, covering her voice, "Glenn Ford's the German, but in this a guy named Pedro hid the gold. It was like $20-million worth. And Apaches had killed Pedro. That's all made up. That's not really the legend. In this, though, Apaches killed Pedro because he buried gold in the home of their thunder god or something. It's a weird angle really."

She tried to stand so I struck her again. I followed her to the ground after that, going to my knees. I rummaged her pockets, found the switchblade, and then I pulled it out. I sprung open the knife. I shoved Anna onto her back. Her face was mottled blue like she was having a heart attack. Maybe it was a stroke. Maybe it was the heroin.

"In case you're wondering, Ford never finds the gold," I said. "He gets damn close. Son of a bitch opposing him gets bitten by a snake, falls off the side of a cliff. It's crazy."

I pulled her away from the Cadillac. I wanted enough distance between Anna and the car so that she didn't get blood on the door. You always see cops scraping flakes of blood off cars in the movies. I didn't want that.

She was still conscious. She looked up at me, but I'm not sure how much she saw. Despite the moon, it was dark in the desert. I don't know if it was the blow to the ear or not, but blood filled her tear ducts.

I put away the blackjack and gripped the knife.

"You know they filmed some of that out here in the mountains," I said. I started laughing, thinking about the guy falling off the cliff in the movie. Me and Dom mocked that scream for a week. It was a good memory. It was the way our life should be.

Anna didn't scream like that, not even with the first entry of the blade. Her brain was too bruised. She gasped and moaned. When she raised her hand, I cut that, too.

The mountains weren't visible from the distance, but I looked at the desert and thought, *Dom and I will hike out here, too. There are so many things we haven't done. So many things.*

I kept at it with the switchblade until my arm was weak.

CHAPTER EIGHTEEN

I made good time on Route 60 back to Snowflake. It was all accomplished under the cover of night. At one juncture, when I was cruising a straight stretch at ninety miles per hour with the windows down and The Beach Boys' "I Get Around" blasting on the radio, I experienced a moment of euphoria. The world came together at a pinpoint of the sublime, and the feeling washed over me as I crossed through it. Anna had lived in my head for a decade plus. That part of my life was over forever. Anna was dead. Newt was dead. Graf would die in prison.

Judging from my mother's letters, she would soon die, too. I'd been mortified when I read the state was transferring her from prison to an asylum. I figured the next step was getting booted to the curb, but thank God, my mother was too gone to be free.

Everyone wrapped up. Everyone buried.

Except for a break at a 24-hour truck stop bathed in fluorescence, where I filled the tank, washed up in the men's room, changed clothes, retrieved my jacket and jewelry from the trunk, and bought a coffee from a sweet old lady named Deloris at the counter, I didn't drop below eighty miles per hour. I rode the entire way with the windows down, all four of them, to get Anna's stink out of the Cadillac. To a degree, it worked, but her odor had mileage. I kept the Top Forty station on until the signal faded. After that I let white noise play low.

When I pulled into Saint Paul's ranch, the sky was purpling, but the sun had yet to rise. I saw people lying around the knoll behind the ranch house like a massacre had taken place. From this distance, I couldn't tell if Dominic was among them. The three junkies stood outside the barn, close to where I'd left them, watching the gate. I waved at them as I rolled down the driveway. They didn't return the gesture, although one of them started to follow my car.

In that moment, I was the essence of untroubled joy. I had nothing to hide.

I'd left the switchblade in Anna's open gut. I'd discarded my shirt and gloves on a trail near her body, hoping these things would give the appearance that the killer had run naked into the desert. The blackjack was clean and in the glove box. I was clean. The car was clean.

I'd even beaten Karl Landrum's arrival at the commune. No new automobiles occupied the lot.

I locked up everything and headed inside. The junkie who followed went to my trunk and tried it a few times. I chased him off by throwing gravel at him. Like a dog, he scuttled back to the barn.

That's not heroin, I thought, watching him go. I had the idea Saint Paul was injecting bleach into their brains, but that was his business.

A few people lay in the front room, huddled in a sleeping mass on the floor. Morning cartoons played on the television. I slipped past them, keeping my footfalls soft. I stepped into the bedroom that was reserved for me and Dom. To my relief, he wasn't inside. The room was dark, quiet, and empty. I looked out the window. Among the rabble, I found him. He slept at the base of the knoll with a silly grin on his face. Luna was at his feet, holding his guitar as she slept. The fire was mostly embers and smoke. No light came from it. It hadn't been fed for a few hours.

I was too tired to do much thinking, or to go out and retrieve Dom, but I felt grand. A weight was lifted from my shoulders.

What about Landrum?

I'll deal with him tomorrow, I thought, and that was that.

With a smile that rivaled Dom's, I stripped one of the nasty mattresses clean, leaving the pillow and piss stains. With my clothes on, and my shirt untucked, I stretched out. I was asleep in minutes. I didn't see the sun come through the window.

CHAPTER NINETEEN

I awoke to Dom sitting on the end of the mattress, playing his guitar, strumming chords and humming. I creased my cemented eyelids. He had the curtains drawn and the window open. Painful sunlight filled the room. A wave of nausea hit me, and a sharp headache had my skull throbbing. I removed my wrist from under the pillow and looked at my watch. I squinted until the numbers came into focus. It was a quarter to ten in the morning.

When Dominic caught me stirring, he turned. He was wearing another of his loud, Hawaiian shirts.

I groaned, burying my face in the pillow. The pounding moved around my head like a worm.

On the floor, Dom slid a mirror with a single line of coke. He pushed it toward my head. "I saved you that," he said.

I got to my elbow. I wiped crust from my eyes.

"Do we have any water?" I asked. I wanted to be home. I wanted to be awakened by Ardella's claws.

Dominic put down his guitar and stepped around the room, searching. He came back with a can of Blatz, a third full. There weren't alternatives, and I didn't want to see Saint Paul's people yet, so I took it. I drank the hot, flat swill with a single gulp. The beer was rancid, but it was enough to wet my mouth. Before my nausea shot the beer back up, I did the line Dom saved for me.

Dominic snickered at my ineptitude.

"Have to claw the boogers out of your nose first," he said.

I didn't care. I put my head back on the pillow and stared at the ceiling. For a second, my head and eyes were on fire. When I was sure I wouldn't vomit, I pinched the remaining powder from my nostrils. The coke started to work on my brain after a few minutes, and the throbbing subsided.

"Where'd you go last night?" Dominic asked. He lifted his guitar and placed it on his thigh. His left hand moved over the frets.

I closed my eyes to block out light. "Close the curtains," I muttered.

He didn't close the curtains. Instead, he played through a song, humming the lyrics rather than singing, and then he asked me again.

"Where'd you go?"

"What are you talking about?" I asked. I yawned and wiped at my nose. Powder stuck like a web.

"A chick named Sabina came in here lookin' for you. Said you flipped out and left last night. You had her worried."

"Oh," I said. "Do you want to know the truth?"

Dom stopped playing.

"I had to get away from her. She was on me like Luna's been on you."

Dominic nodded, but his satisfaction was insincere.

I resented his suspicion.

"I drove out to get a pack of cigarettes to get free of Sabina. I stayed in here when I got back."

"She said she couldn't find you. She looked."

I felt his eyes on me.

"That was by design," I said. I attempted a smile.

"You don't seem like you got much sleep," he said pointedly.

"I didn't. I was at the window watching you most of the night."

"You weren't with Sabina? You promise?"

"Dom…"

He sighed. "Fine. Did you see what happened?"

"Terrestrially, nothing happened."

"Man, they said there were lights all night."

"Just shooting stars."

"That's it?"

"That's it."

Dom lit a cigarette. He pulled another out of the smashed pack in my pocket, and then he lit it for me. He tucked it in my mouth. It was one of the nonfilters I bought at the truck stop.

"You're supposed to be smoking kings," he chided.

"Stress," I said.

I inhaled deeply, and that did more to cure me than anything. I smoked greedily. I hated coke. I don't know why I did it. The coke replaced my nausea with creeping sickness. I'd regret it for the remainder of the day.

Dominic played the guitar some more. He started on "Mr. Spaceman" by The Byrds. He grinned at me.

"How come you're not telling me about your trip?" I asked. I flicked ash onto the floorboards. "Goddamn coke," I said, feeling dizzy.

Over chords, Dom said playfully, "What do you think happened?"

I focused on the gutted light fixture in the ceiling.

"I figure your soul came out of your nose like steam, and you were assumed into the mothership."

"Well, that's the official line," Dom said. He laughed. "Apparently, that happened to the others. I told 'em it was too blurry for me to remember. Saint Paul said it was too heavy for me to remember, that I was blocking it to protect myself. He said I was in the ship, too, though. He saw me."

I laughed with him. "He saw you in the waiting room," I said.

"On a slab. We were all laid out on slabs below an altar. Saint Paul was on the altar."

"Of course."

"You know what really happened?"

"What?"

"Jack shit," Dom whispered. He adjusted his glasses. "I saw a bug with pincers crawl out of the sand at one point, but it walked into the fire and burned up. It was about the size of a puppy. It screamed."

"That's horrifying," I said.

He didn't like the look on my face. "Don't say it. Don't you dare, Royce."

"What if that was one of the aliens?"

Dom smacked my leg. "Don't be a bastard," he said. "I don't want that to pop in my head next time I'm alone. There were no aliens."

"That's not how we're going to tell it today," I said. I sat up fully. My back and shoulders hurt down in the nerves. My headache ebbed, but I still felt like shit. "Is there a place to clean up?" I asked.

"A shower stall outside. Like at the beach."

"Fantastic." I put my head on the pillow. "I wonder how the Mormons feel about that?"

"Did you really go get cigarettes last night?" Dom asked. "That all?"

"That's all," I said. "I'd never lie to you, Dom. Sabina was spaced out. She lost track of me is all. Thank Christ."

"I know you don't," Dom said. "You look different, though."

"Feeling better about it all," I said.

He didn't say anything.

"That bug screaming," I said, "you know what that reminds me of? Remember when we watched *Lust for Gold* on the sofa, and that guy fell off the cliff screaming at the end? Remember us laughing about that?"

Dominic thought for a moment. He shook his head. "No," he said, chuckling.

"Sure you do. It had Glenn Ford in it. It was about the Lost Dutchman's Mine. We laughed about it for a week," I said. "A snake bit the guy, and he fell off a cliff, screaming."

"Maybe you and Ardella," Dom said. "I never watched that with you. I've never seen it."

I blew a cloud of smoke through my nostrils, trying to clear them. "Sure you did," I said, smiling at the memory.

"Did you cut yourself last night?" Dom asked.

"I don't think so. Why?"

"There's a big drop of blood on the toe of your shoe."

"Wasn't me. There's no telling around here." I looked at the ceiling. "No telling what drips through these ceilings."

"I mean a *big* splash," Dom said. He looked up.

"No telling," I repeated, swinging my legs from the soiled mattress.

"One of the junkies said the Cadillac didn't pull back into the lot until morning, Royce."

The tone left me angry, but I fought it.

"I didn't know the zombies talked. One of them said that to you?"

"Not me. One of 'em told Sabina. She told me."

"I see. She's a troublemaker, too, then, isn't she? You trying to be a troublemaker, Dom? Is that what you're going for?" I left my gaze on him. I left it there until he turned to the window.

"I guess she's full of shit," Dom said.

"She's fucking spaced out," I said. "She saw aliens last night, too, didn't she?"

Dom nodded. "I cleaned your shoe," he said absently.

CHAPTER TWENTY

After Dominic connected a fresh reel on the tape recorder, I turned to Saint Paul. He reclined on the divan in his holy of holies, smoking a joint. The air was pungent. I pulled a chair to the coffee table. I sat near his head like a psychiatrist.

Through a cloud of smoke, Saint Paul watched Dom with a look of disappointment.

"Neither of you made it with the chicks I sent you last night," he observed. He looked at me with similar displeasure. "What gives, man?"

"We're professionals," I said.

He took a drag on the joint. He smiled at that, but he frowned at me.

"Man, are they not your types? Is that it?"

"It isn't that, at all," I said. "We simply don't mix business with pleasure. I take this work quite seriously." I gestured at the alien face on his wall. "After Dominic's experience, one I believe he's buried, I want to get to the bottom of things. Perhaps then we can enjoy what you have to offer."

"Okay, Doc. Fair enough. So, what are we recording?"

"The recording will be a documentation of the session," Dominic said. "You'll receive transcriptions of all recordings."

"How much do you charge for the tapes, brother?" Saint Paul asked.

"If you have facilities for making duplicates, we'll entertain that at no charge," I said. "We keep the originals, though."

He worked on the joint. "Science, man," he said. "Y'all are a couple scientists, man. Does it get complicated?"

"Actually, it's a simple process," I said. "One in which you must cooperate to be successful. You can't hypnotize someone against their will. There's no magic to it."

"That's good to know, man."

"You were worried about that?"

He smoked.

"All that's needed is an object to fixate on. With that, you'll be lulled into a trancelike state, one in which you're conscious of your surroundings." I gestured around the room. "None of this will go away. You're not going to be on another plane of existence. You'll be here. You'll feel the sofa beneath you. You're simply going to open yourself to suggestion. It will feel like the twilight between waking and sleep. Through my suggestions, you'll push aside barriers and get at a deeper level of memory."

Saint Paul looked at me sincerely. "I don't want you askin' about the war, man. Don't dig in there, you understand?"

"We won't broach the war," I promised.

"Alright, Doc, I trust you. Promise me one more thing, man."

"What's that?" I asked.

"Don't tell anybody what I say without my permission. And don't play those tapes for anybody, man. Not anybody."

"Everything said in this room is confidential," I reassured him. I leaned back to Dom. "Will you get me another cup of coffee?" I asked. I handed him my empty mug.

He took it, nodding.

"That's chicory, brother," Saint Paul explained. "Chicory gets in your head in a different way than coffee, doesn't it? The chicory plant's blue like the sky. Make of that what you will."

"Fascinating," I said.

Saint Paul nodded. "Has an earthy bouquet."

"Uh-huh."

"A nutty nose."

"Okay."

"A ribald *je ne sais quois.*"

"Sure."

Saint Paul licked his fingers, pinched out the joint, tucked it away, and grinned at me.

Dominic returned with two cups of *chicory*. He handed mine over.

"Alright, brother," Saint Paul said. "Time to get serious. No more jokes."

He stretched out on the divan, his bare feet hanging over the end. He lay back and crossed his hands on his stomach. He wore rings made of braided hair. I didn't particularly want to know where the rings originated, so I didn't ask.

I drank the chicory and placed the cup on the table. I scooted the chair closer to the divan. My head was clearer than it had been all day. The morning headache was gone. The Landrums hadn't shown.

Saint Paul opened one eye as if he read my mind.

"You think Landrum will show?" he asked.

"Karl Landrum's a sad man," I told him. "He'll show."

Saint Paul took a deep breath.

"I want you to relax," I began. "Keep breathing. I want you to breathe deeply. I want you to enter a state of complete and total relaxation."

With a click, Dom switched on the tape recorder.

I spoke slightly louder than the whir of the machine, but my tone lost all edge. Softly, I said, "Listen to my voice. I want you to open your eyes."

Saint Paul cooperated. With a sigh, he opened his eyes.

I held a crystal pendulum on a golden chain. I moved it back and forth a couple feet from his nose.

"I want you to focus on a particular color within the crystal," I said. "I want you to find the color you find most soothing. Fixate on that color. Don't lose it as the pendulum moves. Follow it. Follow my voice. Follow the color. You're going to bypass the conscious mind. You're going to move into the unconscious mind. Don't lose the color. Watch it. Don't lose the color."

Saint Paul followed the crystal with rapt attention.

"When your eyes tire," I said, "when you can no longer hold them open, I want you to close them. Allow the lids to fall. Close them."

Dominic and I had a routine worked out for sessions without an audience. When I raised the index finger of my left hand, he switched off the recorder. When I raised the index and middle finger together, he switched it back on. The gaps in the recording allowed for suggestions. I planted ideas in the lacunae.

For the next hour, Saint Paul discussed extraterrestrials and abductions. Some of the discussion came from his imagination, and some of it came from mine. I led him where I wanted things to go. We explored the interior of the ship (I allowed too much *Star Trek* into that), the texture and scent of the beings (I allowed Betty and Barney Hill into that), and we talked about the Gaelic tongue, which was, I supposed, unique to Saint Paul's cult. In a moment of inspiration, one in which Dom stopped the tape, I asked if the aliens had told him about the Irish legend of *Connla and the Fairy Maiden*. It was a tale I'd cribbed from my library reading, and it fit the cult's mythos. Saint Paul said he didn't remember. I told the story of the hero Connla, his beguiling encounter with an ethereal woman, and his departure from this earthly plane with the mysterious fairy maiden. I framed the tale as a question, and then I raised two fingers.

The reel whirred.

I asked Saint Paul to repeat what he remembered of the tale, suggesting the extraterrestrials told him the legend.

He became visibly agitated, trying to recall when the face on the wall had told him such a thing.

I talked him down, reassured him, and then I repeated my request.

It clicked. Growing excited, Saint Paul said, "She sees me as Connla of the Fiery Hair, son of Conn of the Hundred Fights. That was her back then, man. That was her coming out of the water, climbing the shore. She's the maiden. Where have I heard that before?"

"Did she tell you the legend? Is that where you learned the names?"

"She says she's the Fairy Maiden. She visited Connla back then. She's visiting me now."

"She told you the legend, didn't she?"

"Yes," Saint Paul said.

"You've never read it? It's not something you've carried from childhood?"

"No. She told me. She says it's like *Genesis*. She says I'll write the next *Genesis*."

"What does she want?" I asked.

"To escort my people to the *Moy Mell*."

"I've never heard that term, Saint Paul. Is that in the legend? What is Moy Mell?" I asked.

"The plains of pleasure, man," he said wistfully. "Heaven, brother. It's part of the legend she told me. No, not legend, man. History. I was on the altar. She was above me. She was whispering in my ear. She doesn't breathe when she speaks. It's telepathic. Still, I got chills. She escorted Connla there in a silver canoe. Goddamn, that's a fuckin' rocket, man. She'll escort me."

I caught Dominic shaking his head, smiling behind the recorder.

"The plains of pleasure," I repeated. "Has she promised to take you to Moy Mell?"

Saint Paul's mind went to work on what I'd told him. He built on it.

"Only when we're ready," he said. "When we're ready she'll take my people there." That was all him.

"One day your body will go up instead of your soul? You'll be assumed in a beam of fire."

"One day," he said breathlessly. "One day our bodies will go up instead of our souls. We'll be assumed in a beam of fire."

"I want you to repeat the legend in Gaelic, as you first absorbed it telepathically."

Saint Paul rambled in gibberish for a couple minutes. It was a struggle, but I kept a straight face. I didn't know a word of Gaelic, but there was no framework to the "language" he spoke. The only connecting tissue was the prefix *mac* thrown in every few words. Pig Gaelic, as it were. Moved by the Holy Spirit, Saint Paul kept at it, blathering.

I looked at Dominic. He had his eyes closed, concentrating, trying not to laugh.

"Repeat the legend in English," I said.

Saint Paul started again, painting a portrait of the fiery-headed Connla on the shore with his father so long ago, watching a being approach from the stars.

"Are you a reincarnation of Connla?" I asked.

He liked that. Hesitantly, he nodded.

"Does she want you to assume this name, Connla, rather than Saint Paul?"

I shrugged at Dominic.

"She wants me to take the name, Connla," said Saint Paul. "That's what she's been trying to tell me."

He opened his eyes suddenly. "I have to gather my people," he said. "Doc, I have to gather my people."

I patted his shoulder.

Dominic stopped the tape.

"That's enough for now," I said. "Try to relax. Take a breath. You did well."

"Get Hazel and Celeste in here," Saint Paul said. "Please, Doc."

Dominic stood and moved to the door.

"We're getting them," I said. "Be calm. Breathe."

"Doc, I feel like a revelator writing revelations."

"Can I play the tape back for you?" I asked. "It got heavy. You need to hear it." I showed him the chill bumps on my arms.

Saint Paul sat up. "Yeah, it's foggy, though. I wanna hear it in full."

As I fiddled with the reel, Dominic returned with Hazel and Celeste, both full of concern.

"It's all joy," Saint Paul reassured them. He patted the divan. "Everything's good. I want you to bear witness."

The guardians obeyed, taking a seat on either side of their leader.

CHAPTER TWENTY-ONE

With a revelation too important to conceal, Saint Paul called together his flock for an emergency sermon on the knoll. With the Connla legend, and he himself at the center of it, he had a new framework for the religion he was building. Saint Paul couldn't hold his excitement, not even long enough for me to go through the rest of my subjects. I'd only conducted sessions with he, Celeste, and Hazel thus far, but Saint Paul halted any further hypnosis until everyone on the ranch knew what he knew about Connla. He agreed to pay us and let us vacate the ranch early, with the agreement that we'd return for further sessions soon. He wanted time to chew on the new angle (and work it into his manuscript) before continuing. He gave me an envelope of cash as payment. That was fine with me.

While his brethren herded everyone together for the sermon, a green Mercury pulled through the front arch and started down the driveway. The car moved too fast for the amount of people around. The driver honked to clear a path.

Dominic and I stood on the front porch, taking in some sun, leaning on columns, and smoking. I checked my watch. It was after four p.m. We had to be on the road soon if we wanted to make it back to the city before dark.

The Mercury was a late model Cougar, a two-door coup. A layer of dust covered it from a long drive. The shine was gone. As the car neared, I glimpsed the driver through the windshield. He was looking at me, too. Animated, he gestured at the crowd of people in his wake.

It was Karl Landrum, eight hours behind his time. His wife, Shea, rode in the passenger seat, calm and prim. If Karl wanted a debate, he was too late for that. I was too tired to deal with his shit. He'd have to wait until next time.

"Here we go," Dominic said, tensing. He flicked ash from his cigarette. "We should've left an hour ago."

I smiled at him. "Everything packed up?" I asked.

Dom nodded. "I cleared out the room."

"Tape recorder?"

"Got it."

We stayed in place as the Mercury pulled to a stop behind the three-wheeled truck. Then, as if they'd been hiding in a pile of garbage, a couple junkies rushed into the lot like lunatics. It was amusing to watch the ordeal from this angle, without the anxiety of besiegement. A man and woman, the same pair that accosted us, went to the Landrum's trunk and worked on it, shoving it down, lifting it up. The back end of the car rose and fell on the shocks.

"Fuck's sake," Dominic said. He laughed.

Unlike Dom and I, Karl Landrum showed no patience. He flung open his door. His outfit was something else: a yellow turtleneck tucked into red, pinstriped pants. The pants were so tight I saw the head of his circumcised penis.

"You have to be kidding," Dom said.

Landrum stood straight in the gravel, pointing at the man and woman prying his trunk. He flung some invectives. He went big and small with those, but nothing landed. While

Shea waited safely inside, Karl berated the junkies until his face was red. The zombies didn't notice his presence. Giving Karl the cold shoulder, the man worked his fingers under the lip of the trunk. He heaved like he was lifting a log off a loved one, his back arching with strain. The woman thumped metal.

Luna sprinted in from the barn, her wild hair bouncing. She cut through a crowd of onlookers.

"You know what would be a gas?"

"What's that?" Dom asked.

"If the junkies killed Karl." I laughed at the thought of it. "If only," I said. "Run down and suggest it before Luna saves him."

Dominic didn't find the idea humorous. He gave me a side-eye.

"I suppose we should greet the bastard," I conceded.

We reached the lot just as Luna arrived. Barking Spanish, she chased away the zombies. Luna told them to go inside and take their "medicine." They did as they were told.

The small crowd of Saint Paul's followers moved closer to us, forming an audience. I looked around for their leader, but he wasn't among them. I figured he was prepping on the knoll.

I approached Karl Landrum with confidence. Why not? His weapon was gone. I'd castrated him. I wanted to lord over him and watch him squirm. Gingerly, Shea stepped from the car. She watched me. Karl watched me. I sensed they were nervous. I hadn't gotten that feeling from them on New Year's Eve, so I liked it.

"Dr. Landrum," I said, extending my hand. "What a surprise."

He considered not shaking it, but he gave me a limp

return, quick and done. The inclusion of "doctor" didn't jar him, but he shot back.

"Mr. Pembrook," he said.

We played the game. "This is my partner, Dominic," I offered.

Dom nodded, but he didn't shake hands. Instead, he tipped his yellow sunglasses and, rudely, blew clove smoke at Landrum.

Landrum brushed the smoke from his face. "*Partner*," he repeated with disgust. "Yes, he looks it."

"Mrs. Landrum," I said across the top of the car. "How do you do?"

Shea nodded. "Mr. Pembrook," she said.

"It's Madigan," I corrected.

"Oh, yes," Karl said. "Our mistake."

Luna returned with a smile on her face. It was too bright to be real. She'd collected it from her pocket somewhere between the car and the ranch-house door. She didn't greet Karl like she'd greeted Dom because Saint Paul hadn't given her orders to screw him.

"Who are you?" she asked Karl directly.

"Why, this is Dr. Karl Landrum, associate of the APRO," I said. "They're critics of this place, you know. Saint Paul requested his presence. Like a good vassal, here he is, summoned."

Landrum glared at me.

Uncertain, Luna said, "Stay here. Let me find Paul." Flustered, she turned to go.

"I'm afraid you missed the show," I said. "Last night and this morning."

Shea walked around the front of the car, joining us.

"You won't be so glib when I tell you why we're late," Karl

said. He wore a brown leather jacket over the turtleneck. He gripped the lapels as he spoke. It was the only way he kept from jamming his finger in my face.

"I can't be bothered with such details," I said. "That's your business. We were getting ready to head out."

"Anna was killed," Shea interjected, as if she didn't want to lose the moment. She watched me for a reaction.

I looked at her, but I checked my emotion. I greeted the news with a blank face. Beside me, I felt Dominic's tension rise.

"A hazard of living on the street. What happened?" I asked calmly.

"We were at the police station for several hours this morning, Pembrook," Karl said.

"Don't tell me they suspect you?"

He shook his head. "No, I identified the body. They don't know what happened. I suggested they speak to you. I'm certain you can expect them when you get home."

"She was stabbed," Shea added. "Many times. She was propped against a stone on the side of the highway."

Watching traffic, I thought, remembering.

Defensively, Dom cut in. "Royce was here with me all night."

"I don't mind calling on the police myself. I'll give them whatever assistance is needed. Poor Anna. That's terribly unfortunate. She was ill, you know?"

"You're not at all relieved to hear it, I suppose?" Karl asked.

"Why would I have a problem with Anna Vogel?" I asked. "I feel nothing but pity for the woman. She was mentally ill. Please don't tell me you had some type of arrangement with her." I looked at Shea. "I don't believe you'd approve of that, would you? Do you realize the type of woman Anna was?"

I shook my head. "She was one step away from that couple prying your trunk."

Saint Paul came through the front door of the ranch house. The screen door slammed shut behind him. He hopped off the porch and traipsed over. Pulling back his hair into a ponytail, he said, "Doc Landrum, you missed the show, man. It's all done now." He patted my shoulder. "Doc Madigan worked his wonders. He found somethin' *mysterious*, man."

"His name is Pembrook, and he certainly isn't a doctor," Karl said. "I've told you that."

I looked at Saint Paul and shrugged. Landrum had a hard sell with a man who dubbed himself "Saint."

"I think the universe hates you," Saint Paul said, "but, man, I'm gonna invite you to my sermon anyway."

"I don't—"

"—Right now," Saint Paul said. He put his arm around Landrum's shoulder. He looked at the crowd. "Let's go, everybody."

Karl wriggled free. "Don't touch me, sir," he said. "I came here to see Mr. Pembrook. I don't give two shits about your goddamn, illiterate sermon."

"Whoa now, brother. If you wanna hear what happened, then come along. If you don't wanna hear, then fuck off, man."

"I don't want to hear any of it." Karl pointed at me. He couldn't help it. "The police will be waiting on you," he said. "I'll make certain of it."

"Why do you think I had anything to do with Anna?" I asked.

As Saint Paul and his people watched, Karl turned to get back in his car.

"I really only wanted to see if you were here," Karl said, and a note of frustration entered his voice.

"It hurt to see me on the porch, didn't it?"

He didn't answer that. He and Shea got back into the Mercury.

"Anna's dead," Dom muttered.

"Truly unfortunate," I said. "That poor woman."

Dominic looked at me for a few seconds longer than natural.

"You fellas be safe on the road," Saint Paul said to us. "And, man, I want you back here soon."

I shook his hand. "Why don't you come down to see me for a session?" I offered.

"Brother, you got it," he said.

Karl backed the Mercury into the crowd. Reluctantly, the flock parted.

When the Mercury gained the road, Saint Paul led his people to the knoll.

"You really think Anna's dead?" Dom asked.

"I don't think he'd lie about something like that."

"Goddamn pigs are gonna show up at our door."

"Probably."

You keep telling them I was with you all night, I thought. *That's a good start.*

"You were with me all night, weren't you?"

I looked hurt. "You know I was, Dom. Don't do that to me."

CHAPTER TWENTY-TWO

By the time I pulled to the curb outside Theda's building, it had been dark for an hour.

Dominic was quiet and morose in the passenger seat. He'd done more thinking than talking during the drive. I wasn't certain what went on inside his head, but I didn't like it. His worry was clear, as was his exhaustion. Periodically, he switched 8-tracks, but he wouldn't bite whenever I used the lull to gauge his doubt. He shrugged away my questions. My resentment grew each time he did.

I threw a cigarette into the gutter and followed Dominic to the entrance. A doorman, one I hadn't seen before, took our names and called up to Theda. When she gave the okay, he opened the door and escorted us to the elevator. We traveled seven floors. Unlike the building in which the Dupreys lived, Theda's was in an older part of the city. It was an elegant but worn place. The elevator, a cage with Egyptian designs in the metal, creaked upward. The lines ticked at each increment.

Dominic stood quietly at my side. We were alone beneath a fluorescent bulb.

"Anna was able to get up to Theda's place. I wonder how she got past the doorman?" I asked.

Dominic cleared his throat. He ran his fingers through his hair. Finally, feeling my tension, he shrugged.

"Why aren't you talking?" I asked.

He frowned. "I'm just tired," he said.

While I looked at him, Dominic stared ahead. He wouldn't allow our eyes to connect.

When the door opened, we walked the corridor to Theda's apartment. We passed a few doors with televisions on the other side, but the floor was fairly quiet. A window at the end was black.

I knocked. After a beat of silence, the burglar chain receded, and a few locks came undone. Theda's face appeared in the door, as did Ardella's nose at the level of my ankles. Theda opened the door wide when I went to a knee for the cat.

"Welcome home, dears," Theda said.

I let out an exaggerated sigh. "Good to see you," I said, looking up.

Dom stood with his hands in his pockets. "Thank you for keeping the baby," he said.

Ardella came into my arms, purring. It was wonderful to be in her presence again. Cradling the cat, I stood.

"Come inside before the others run out," Theda said.

"How are you?" I asked, stepping into an antechamber lit by a small lamp. "Did Anna ever come back?" I placed Ardella on the hardwood floor when she got restless. She had her claws out. She joined three other felines standing in the mouth of a dark hallway that led to Theda's bedroom.

Theda shook her head. Her eyes were red like she'd been reading by lamplight. She was stressed. She had nothing of the devil-may-care attitude she usually possessed.

"All clear." She forced a smile.

"No more telephone calls?"

"None." She looked at Dominic and frowned. "Why the mean mug, darling? Don't tell me you two are having a lovers' quarrel. I couldn't bear it."

"Just tired," Dom said. He didn't smile, and he didn't laugh.

I disliked his attitude, and now he was embarrassing me by being curt with Theda.

"Come," said Theda. "I was just putting on some tea."

We followed to the kitchen, past a wall of framed posters for several films in which Theda had played. There was a single poster of another variety here that I always found curious. It was for a burlesque occult show in 1923 Berlin. That was one story Theda never told. She always deflected when I asked.

Theda switched on the overhead light and the kitchen brightened. Seven cats streamed in, covering the tiled floor. Theda ignored their pleading, placing a kettle on the gas stove. The range, like the Coolerator, was a pastel green.

Dominic started to pull back one of the wooden chairs at the table, but Theda stopped him. "Have a seat in the parlor," she said.

"Theda, I'd love to stay—"

"—But nothing," she cut him off. "I have something I must discuss with both of you." She looked at me kindly. "Go make yourself comfortable, dear. I'll bring the tea."

We did as we were told. I lifted Ardella from the pride, hugging her to my chest, and then I found my way to the parlor.

The room was sumptuous with pillows, deep chairs, shelves of books, framed photographs, Expressionistic paintings, and heavy curtains embroidered with silk. Beneath the curtains, two windows were open to allow in night air. Save for a television cabinet on the floor, the room was a recreation of something the vamp knew a half century prior. There was something Victorian in the room's overstuffed closeness. Unlike Addy and Florinda, Theda had no desire for modern styles.

On the television, a bland figure relayed the Phoenix news in a monotone that matched his looks. The man sat at a desk with a wall of clocks behind him.

I tried to catch Dominic's eye, but he wouldn't play along. Instead, he walked to the chair nearest the television, sat, and turned up the volume with a knob on the box. The anchor's voice moved through the apartment. The story was about a protest of Dow Chemical for making napalm.

I sat on the opposite side of the room. I placed Ardella on my lap. She rubbed her face on my clothes, purring loudly.

After a couple minutes, Theda returned with a tray. It was odd to see her behave domestically, with her usual vulgarity stripped. She poured tea for three. I took mine with a touch of cream. I stirred it in, conscious not to allow the spoon to touch the sides of the cup. Theda had class enough to notice such things. Dominic, on the other hand, rapped spoon against china, clinking maladroitly.

I was one step from venting my rage at him, audience or not. I breathed to calm myself, focusing on Theda.

She switched on a third lamp and took her place in a seat of worn velvet. The cats, of which I counted eight, crowded at her slippered feet.

"I know," she said.

That was it. She put it out there and let it settle. She oscillated her gaze between the two of us.

Dominic turned his attention from the television. The tea in his hand steamed.

With a touch of nerves, I sipped the drink. It was painfully hot. I watched Theda over the rim of the cup. When she didn't elaborate, I asked playfully, "What is it that you know?"

"That the woman was killed," Theda said. "The tramp who came to my door. When did you plan to tell me, Royce?"

Ardella hopped from my lap. She walked to Dom and smelled the foreignness, the stray-dog scent, of his trousers. She went to work rubbing away the stench, reclaiming her property. Dom ignored her.

"I was leading up to it," I said. "It isn't exactly what one opens the door with. My understanding is that it was quite grotesque. Vicious work."

Theda smiled. "Don't you want to know how I know, dear?" She drank the tea, but her eyes, ringed carefully in a style from the teens, stayed on me.

"I can guess," I said.

"Was it one of the Landrums?" Dominic asked.

Theda brought down her cup. She giggled. "Your skeptic from the party. Indeed, it was. He telephoned to inform me."

"What else did he tell you?" I asked.

"I assume you can guess that, too. He thinks that *you* did it. Better yet, he *knows* that you did it."

I sighed. "He drove three hours to tell me the same."

Theda put her saucer aside. She bent and lifted one of the cats, a beautiful Persian. Darius, I believe.

"What do you mean?" she asked.

She could sense any man squirming, so her natural tendency to needle came through. The Persian stood proudly on her thigh.

"Karl Landrum is positively mad," I said. "He drove from Phoenix to Snowflake to check on my whereabouts. To say the least, he was disappointed to find me so far from Anna. When did he telephone?"

"About an hour before you arrived."

"So, he's still on about it, regardless," I said. "He'll make it work in his head no matter where I was."

"His wife wants me to go with them to the police," Theda said. "He begged me to tell them all I know about you. And about that night at the Aguirre manor."

"Christ," Dominic said. He placed his tea on top of the television.

I drank the rest of mine and found balance.

"It goes without saying that I had nothing whatsoever to do with the poor woman's death. Doesn't this sort of thing happen to street people daily? Getting murdered every now and then is part of their image."

"Darling, you sound like Florinda. Oh, I don't believe you're capable of such a thing. You're too gentle. I've known brutes, dear. I know how they behave." She paused, allowed a thought to pass. "I am worried about you, though. The man's zealotry for hounding you troubles me."

"I believe Karl Landrum killed Anna to have something to pin on me." I looked across the room at Dominic. "We witnessed his temper today. He's a man capable of great violence, I think. If driven to it."

Dominic nodded. "He's not above it," he said.

"What would drive him to it?" Theda asked.

"Money."

"Why does he hate you so?"

"Someone is paying him to hate me so. When did you last speak with Addy or Florinda?" I asked.

"Yesterday afternoon," Theda said. "Florinda called."

"And what do you know about their brother, Ian Duprey?"

Theda shifted her eyes to the ceiling.

"Oh God, what a bastard Ian is. Positively a pompous, duplicitous ogre of a man. He runs several banks, you know?"

"He runs their bank," I said. "He gives Addy and Florinda allowances."

Theda nodded. "That's because his father was an ogre, too, darling. Ian has always controlled his sisters to a degree. He's always interfered in their lives." Dramatically, she shuddered. "He had to approve their marriages, you know. All of them. I refuse to be in a room with the man. Positively refuse."

"How do Addy and Florinda feel about him?"

"They loathe him properly, of course."

I reclined. "That's good to know," I said. "He's the reason Landrum's after me."

Dom furrowed his brow. "Where'd you learn that?" he asked.

I started to say that Anna told me, but I stopped.

"I lied to you last night," I said. "I wasn't able to speak to Addy or Florinda. I spoke to Ian. He told me directly. I didn't want you to be upset."

Dom cut his gaze to the television screen. He didn't say anything.

"Why would he ever want to keep *you* from his sisters?" Theda asked.

"He believes I'm a conman."

Theda scoffed. "How do you deal with all these skeptics?" she asked sincerely. "Why must they torment you?"

"They're usually not so persistent as this," I said, laughing at the genuineness of her tone. "You know how I feel about Addy and Florinda. They're dear friends. Why would I con them? I love them. I have no reason."

"They pay significantly more money to keep Thibodeaux

and Drucilla than to keep you," Theda agreed. "Ian's simply trying to assert his control over them."

"He'll be after the dogs next," I said.

"I'm sorry to be cruel, darling," Theda said, "but it pleased me to hear that the woman was dead. I don't like to think of her in pain, but I was quite relieved. I thought she was going to shoot her way through my door. She was like a little gun moll. I haven't been outside in two days. She frightened me to that degree, darling."

"Did you mention to Karl that you and I spoke on the telephone last night? That I was at Saint Paul's commune in Snowflake when we did?"

"Certainly, I did," Theda said. "His brusqueness can't fluster me. Mind you, he tried. I can deal with demanding men."

"What time did you say we spoke?"

"I didn't have occasion to mention a specific time. He talks so quickly, you know. He moves from one point to the next."

"Will you do me an important favor, Theda?" I asked. "If the police come calling, will you make our conversation as late in the evening as you reasonably can?"

"Why would I do that?" she asked.

"Because the police are going to take a serious look at me. Karl Landrum will make certain of that. He's already spoken to them. They'll come front loaded."

"If he's to be believed," Dominic said. "He could be bluffing."

"Perhaps," I said, "but I believe him."

"I'll do what I can," Theda said.

"Will you do something else for me?"

Theda scratched the Persian's ear. "Yes," she said quietly.

I stood, and I looked down at her. "Arrange for me to see

Addy and Florinda tomorrow. I can't telephone without running afoul of Ian."

The vamp agreed. "That sort of thing really does happen to street people all the time, Royce dear. It barely makes the news. Don't you worry." She looked at Dominic, smiling. "I couldn't imagine Royce harming anyone," she said. "I've never even seen him angry. Can you imagine such a delicate soul striking another?"

Dominic was silent, tracing lines in the rug on the floor. He struggled to find his loyalty, but he found it.

"Me either," he said finally. "I can't accept that he'd ever be violent."

CHAPTER TWENTY-THREE

For most of the night, Dominic and I were awake in the bedroom. The blankets were at the end of the mattress, kicked into a tangle.

I stared at a window, beneath which Ardella lay curled, sleeping in the crease of a chair. The cat, at least, was happy to be home. My clothes were draped over the chair's arm. I stared at the window until the first rays of sunlight pierced the blinds. My mind was dull with exhaustion.

Dominic hadn't said much all night, so I was surprised when he turned to me. We behaved like we were angry with one another, but neither would break the ice. Until now.

With the side of his face smashed against the pillow, he asked, "Royce, will you be completely honest with me?"

What a way to call someone a liar, I thought. He took the scenic route to get there, but he got there.

I rolled over on my shoulder and looked at him.

He found my hand on the sheets. He took it, gripped it.

"Yes," I said.

The rattle of rain came through the window. The tapping awakened Ardella. She stood and stretched.

"I mean it this time," he said. "You really must be honest with me. It will never leave this room."

I tried not to get angry. I didn't say anything. I watched his eyes.

"Did you have anything at all to do with Anna's death? I mean in any capacity."

I'm losing respect for you, I thought, and the clarity of the idea shook me. I didn't voice the words because they were too painful. I stared through him. I didn't want our relationship to slide downward—the idea frightened me—but I couldn't stop the barrage of thoughts.

Who are you to ask such a thing? Who are you to back me into a corner? Ever? I pulled you out of the gutter, Dominic. You were going nowhere. You were afraid to be yourself. You were ashamed. I pulled you up here with me. I lifted you up.

When have you ever helped me? Now's your chance. I need you. And this is what I get.

I didn't take my eyes off his eyes.

"No," I said in a level voice. "I had nothing at all to do with Anna, Dom. I promise you."

A memory surfaced, the shade of an old mood that had slammed into me once before. *Why can't we be normal, Royce?* Dominic had asked. *I want to be normal. I want a normal life.*

How dare you?

Stop, I begged myself.

If you don't lie for me, Dom, I'll kill you, I thought. A cold beat passed as my mind stilled. *If you ever become something that stands in my way, Dominic, I'll kill you. I love you, but I'll kill you.*

"It's just…seeing what you did at the gas station is sticking with me," Dom said. "I never would've thought…"

"I don't want you to bring that up anymore," I warned. "I don't want to think about it. I don't want to hear about it ever again. It was a mistake. That's all it was. I made a mistake.

They were hurting you, so I made a mistake. It reflects nothing else."

"I…" He let it go.

"You what, Dom?"

"I love you, Royce," Dominic said. He released my hand.

"Good."

Then behave like you love me, I thought. *Stop scrutinizing. Give me what I deserve.*

"Anna being dead benefits you," he continued. "The police will see that."

I turned onto my back. Ardella had leapt onto the mattress. She kneaded the sheets. I poked the cat with my foot, smiling at her.

"Her death hurts me more than it helps," I said. "Look at all the doubt I'm getting. Even you doubt me, and I was with you all night."

Dominic was quiet for a moment, thinking.

"I don't doubt you," he said. "I believe you, Royce. I'm scared is all. Scared for you."

"That's good," I said.

Dominic propped himself on his elbow, listening to a noise above the rain that entered the bedroom like an intruder.

"Is that someone knocking?" he asked.

I quieted my thoughts and listened.

After a moment, three quick raps came from the living room. Then three more.

"Mother of God," Dom said. "Shit."

He jumped out of bed and threw on clothes. Barefoot, and with his Hawaiian shirt unbuttoned, he rushed from the room. Ardella followed.

Feeling the weight of no sleep, I placed my feet on the floor.

A rush of blood became a headache. I was pulling down a shirt when Dominic returned. He looked pale.

"It's two detectives," he said. "They want to talk to you." He rubbed his arm as if he were cold. "What should I tell them?"

I sat on the edge of the bed. I pulled on a pair of socks and shoes. "There's nothing to tell them," I said. I rubbed my skull. I needed a drink—the headache wasn't from lack of sleep. I was in sore need of a drink.

"Give them some coffee, and say I'll be right in."

"You sure?"

I gave Dom a look. "I can't exactly go down the fire escape. They're here. I have to face it."

He left me alone. He padded down the hallway, and then I heard his voice. The front door opened.

The talking was calm, at least. There was no murder squad bottlenecked in our hallway.

I found a hand mirror on the chest of drawers. I straightened what little hair I had, wiped my puffy eyes, and straightened my shirt. I rummaged through the nightstand for a bottle of gin, finding a fifth with a finger's worth at the bottom. I drank what was left. My stomach was on fire, but I gathered myself.

It was okay that I knew about Anna (and it was okay that Landrum had told me), so I walked to the living room with proper gravity. My breath was hard. I tasted it. I extracted a cigarette as I entered the room. With a flick of the lighter, I had the stick burning.

I found Dominic in the kitchen, preparing coffee, and two plainclothes detectives sitting side by side on our sofa. They weighted the cushions down to the floor. They were a somber pair, both wearing dark ties, both night squad. One of the men, with a high-and-tight hairdo, wore a charcoal blazer. The other was in shirtsleeves. His shoulders were wet from walking in the rain. He had his hair combed over in a modern style. A trace of youth endured in his face. He was the reconciler, I figured, while Mister Defense Industry at his side was the ball-breaker.

Dom brought two cups of coffee into the living room. He handed them over. I felt his nerves, so I know the pigs did. Dom hated cops—he believed them all to be murderous fascists. Having two in his living room, drinking his coffee, had to be a low point in his life.

The cops took the coffee like it was an offering. There was no gratitude in the way they accepted it.

"I'm Detective Matson," the one in shirtsleeves said. "This is my partner, Detective Blomquist."

I told them my name. I opened the living-room window, allowing the post rain aroma into the room, and then I sat in a chair that faced the sofa. I flicked ash into the ashtray near my arm. Dominic brought me coffee. He was acting so unnatural that even Ardella thought him a stranger. The cat hid in the kitchen. She climbed into a cabinet. I heard the door open and shut with a pop.

"What are you men doing together at this time of night?" Blomquist asked. A look of disgust accompanied the question. He had opinions. He was the type of guy who discussed politics in church.

"We live together," I said. I rested the cigarette on the ashtray and tasted the coffee. I was hoping to find some gin, but it was straight.

"Why would two men live together, son?" he asked.

"Cost of living crisis," I said. "With all the Angelenos moving into town, it's brutal these days."

His face reddened.

No more of that, I thought. *He'll blow his top.*

Matson, the younger detective, cut in. "Do you know why we're here, Mr. Madigan?"

I didn't say anything. Out of the corner of my eye, I saw Dominic leaning against the kitchen doorway, watching us. He looked like my frightened wife. Blomquist watched him like he was contagious.

Matson proceeded with a longwinded explanation of the circumstances that brought him to my door, and the circumstances that put me under suspicion for the death of Anna Vogel. He struck me as straightforward, but he was too smart to tip his hand.

I gave an equally long-winded explanation of my whereabouts on the night of Anna's death. To my ears, it was airtight.

"How many people do you have who'd be willing to sign an affidavit to that effect?" Blomquist asked.

I listed a few. "Saint Paul and his commune to begin with," I said.

"Is that a cult, sir?" Matson asked.

"Alternative living," I said.

He smirked. "Who else?"

I nodded at the kitchen. "Dominic was with me. While there, I telephoned Theda Eklund, Adelaide Duprey, and Florinda Duprey. If you can track down the operators I spoke with, that'd prove it."

"You phoned all of these individuals while in Snowflake?" Blomquist asked.

I nodded.

"You said Duprey," Matson started. "Are you speaking of *the* Dupreys?"

Like the Aguirre family, the Dupreys were old money.

"The same," I said. "Their brother is Ian Duprey."

Matson shook his head. "That's a good start," he admitted.

"I have more."

"Go ahead."

"Dr. Karl Landrum and Mrs. Shea Landrum saw me on Saint Paul's premises yesterday."

Matson nodded.

"Miss Theda Eklund saw Anna Vogel the day she died. That proves she was alive when I left town."

Blomquist grinned. "Could be that you drove up to Snowflake, drove back down and killed Miss Vogel, and drove up again. It ain't like you traveled to New York, mister." He looked at his partner. "It's what? A couple hours?"

"Closer to three," I said. "Each way." I didn't let Blomquist get me flustered. I sipped the coffee, hands steady.

"Do you drive a beige 1966 Cadillac sedan, sir?" Matson asked.

I kept at the coffee while my cigarette burned in the tray. "I do," I said.

Matson nodded. He pulled a notebook from his pocket and, for the next minute, wrote the names I'd told him. He asked me for telephone numbers. I gave him the numbers I knew. Blomquist stared.

Finally, Matson looked up from his pad. "Aren't you curious why I asked about the car?" he said.

"No," I said.

He raised his eyebrows, and a sardonic expression surfaced.

"Perhaps you should be. A man at the homeless shelter spotted a similar vehicle on the street around the time Anna Vogel was picked up."

"A lot of cars like that in this city," I said. My chest was tightening, though. I fought it.

"We'll get an exact count of beige Cadillacs from the Highway Department by tomorrow," Blomquist said. "Just for kicks, how many do you guess?"

I shrugged.

"You better hope for at least two," he said.

"Would you like to know what else the man at the homeless shelter saw, sir?" Matson asked. "A man standing in the dark can see what's happening in lighted areas and not be seen at all. He's completely concealed. You'd like to know?"

"Yes," I said. It took an iron will to keep the tremble from my voice.

Matson bit the end his pencil and smiled. It was a nice smile, and he liked using it.

"Yeah, I bet you would."

"Sedan Deville's a nice car," Blomquist said. "You girls share it or what?" He stood from the sofa. He was a large man with a beer gut hanging over his belt. He looked around the living room at our décor. "Smells a bit like marijuana in here," he said. He looked at his partner.

Matson smiled. "Not our line," he told me. "You got a lot more to worry about than that."

Blomquist pointed at me. "Don't you go anywhere," he said. "You're gonna be hearin' from us."

Matson stood. "Do you know anyone who'd have reason to harm Anna Vogel?" he asked.

"Karl Landrum," I managed to say. "He was keeping her on heroin. She was paying him in favors."

"Figures," Matson said. "That's about verbatim what he said about you."

"Landrum drives a green Mercury," Blomquist added.

"I know," I said.

Matson and Blomquist started toward the door.

"There's one more thing," Matson said. "Why do you say your name is Madigan when it's Pembrook?"

I didn't answer.

"You don't like that name, do you? We can settle that later," he said.

CHAPTER TWENTY-FOUR

Adelaide and Florinda came around the corner wearing chiffon party dresses, both navy, both floral. Addy was dignified in white gloves. Florinda suffered in the heat. A wide-brimmed hat of white shaded her face, but to no avail. She waved a fan in one hand.

Walking on leash and harness before the sisters were Thibodeaux and Drucilla. Each dog wore a paisley bandana around the neck to sop up drool and give the appearance of outlawry. We were, after all, meeting outside of town at an amusement park called Legend City. Everything here was Wild West and tacky.

The Dupreys knew the park owner, otherwise the dogs wouldn't have been allowed on the premises. Each week Addy and Florinda brought the dogs here to romp through Legend City. Thibodeaux had a taste for sarsaparilla served in the saloon. He had become something of a local celebrity with children. In addition to his bandana, he wore a tiny cowboy hat strapped around his chin. Drucilla, rightly, rejected this look. Her big flat head was bare in the sun.

I wasn't much for crowded places, so this was my first time visiting the park. The sights, sounds, and odors didn't land with me. I'd spent enough time on the fair circuit for two lifetimes. Kitsch places like this brought nothing but bad memories. I wouldn't have visited at all if it weren't for the insistence of Theda. She thought it was a clever way to avoid the hawkish eye of Ian Duprey. He wouldn't suspect that his sisters met with me on their weekly jaunt—and certainly not, of all places, at a children's park.

I had Theda at my side rather than Dominic. Her energy was better. I'd left Dom at home to fret and wring his hands. To medicate his anxiety, we had his dealer bring over barbiturates. He came up with some yellow jackets, which pleased Dom. By now, Dom was stoned on the bed, listening to records.

Theda was trying to cheer me up with tales of trying and failing to bed Tom Mix when we spotted the Dupreys. She'd been in a couple westerns with him. We stood from the bench and waited in the shade.

Children, milling about the concession "corral" to our right, saw the dogs and broke free of their parents.

Addy's voice cut through the throng. "Say bonjour, Thibodeaux."

The children oohed and awed. To their delight, Drucilla flung drool, showering them.

"Why does Addy do this to poor Florinda?" Theda asked. She shook her head. "Matching dresses, my God. What that poor woman puts up with."

Once the parents scattered their children, we joined the Dupreys under a long, cool veranda with ceiling fans. The dogs trembled with excitement, and their tails extended happily. I scratched their ears, one in each hand, while both dogs leaned into my palms. It was good to be in their presence.

"I thought I'd lost you," I said.

Adelaide handed the leash to Theda and hugged me tightly.

"I was so worried about you, Royce," she said. When she looked up at me, she was in tears. She squeezed. "I'm so sorry for what Ian's done. He's a deplorable man."

"Why does he have an issue with me?" I asked. "It's been years. Why now?"

"Bad investments have him auditing us," Addy said. "He told us to give you up a year ago."

I hugged Florinda, too. She was more sullen. Liquor perfumed her breath. She, too, apologized for her brother.

"Where's Dominic?" she asked.

"Nerves have him bedridden," I said simply.

"Is he medicating?"

I nodded. "He's having a difficult time."

We followed Addy and Thib to a table at the far end of the veranda. From here, looking down the lane, I saw a ride called The Lost Dutchman Mine. A man with a white beard and a Gabby Hayes hat stood outside a wooden fence. He plucked his suspenders and barked at children. Like lines of mice, kids funneled in. A mock waterwheel stood over the barker's shoulder, and the mine entrance, foreboding, stood beyond that. Skeletal fingers clutched the doorway.

Is that an omen? I thought.

For a second, I was struck dumb by the sight. It was a bizarre synchronicity. I hadn't known there was such a ride at the park. *Of all the places to meet.* I thought about watching *Lust for Gold* on the sofa with Dominic again, and I thought about Anna in the desert with the sand and scrub rolling out like a carpet before the Superstition Mountains. There were times I wished I was naïve enough to believe my bullshit, and there were times I didn't. For now, I wished I did.

Coincidence or portents, said the hagridden man.

That was an old chestnut from the fair circuit, one we

paddled around to blur lines and play games with worried clients. I don't know where the phrase first originated or who first used it.

Coincidence or portents?

Strange, I thought, *that the phrase should surface. Strange that things should blur when I need everything to be clear.*

Coincidence or portents?

I settled on the former. A strange coincidence.

"Royce," Florinda was saying. "Royce, are you okay?"

"I want to visit the mine," I said quietly, absently.

Dominic says he doesn't remember watching the movie, but I refuse to believe that. We laughed about that scream for a week. I remember it vividly.

He's an addict, I realized. All that garbage is beginning to erase his memory.

Or he's gaslighting me. Remember that movie, Gaslight?

Yes, I thought. *In my business you must have a good memory.*

Theda and Adelaide looked at one another with concern.

I shook off the feeling, and I returned to the moment. I watched the sisters and Theda.

"I need help," I said flatly.

I took out a cigarette and lit it. I sat on a bench with my back against a wall. The siding was rough and splintered. I was so tired I leaned on it, regardless.

Addy, Florinda, Theda, Thib, and Drucilla surrounded me in a protective crescent.

I told them what Ian Duprey was doing to me. He was not only blocking me from seeing his sisters, which they knew, but he was trying to ruin my life, which they did not know. I told them about his connection to the Landrums. Karl and Shea were skeptics for hire. I told them about Ian's connection to Anna Vogel. Lastly, I revealed my suspicion: Ian wanted me in prison for the murder of Anna.

"I had nothing at all to do with that," I said. "It doesn't look good, though. Your brother and Landrum made it to where it looks bad."

Florinda lifted the skirt of her dress. She drew out a thin flask pinioned to her leg with a garter.

"Put that away," Addy said, jarred. "You're going to get us kicked out."

"It's Miss Kitty realism," Florinda said. She twisted the cap and handed the flask to me. "You can finish it," she said.

I took it. The flask smelled of perfume and sweat, but she was correct in handing it over. After the burst of talking, I needed it. I drank it down. It was fine gin—not the bargain stuff I kept on hand.

"It's only water in a canteen," Florinda told a staring child. "Gotta carry a canteen in the desert."

"Jesus," Theda said.

"Thank you," I said.

"How can we help you, Royce?" Addy asked.

I told them about the police, about their suspicion, about what I believed to be a bluff with the Cadillac. The detail was too specific, I felt. People on the street, in the dark, don't note make, model, year, and color. That tip, if not fabricated, came from Landrum. I was convinced of that. I wouldn't let Matson and Blomquist bully me into tipping my hand. In reality, they had nothing but Karl Landrum running his mouth. Killers greased street people every day.

"We could poison Ian," Florinda suggested. She looked at her sister. "Don't you dare look at me like that. We've certainly discussed it. You even—"

Addy closed her eyes in frustration. "Never say that again," she said.

"I spoke to Theda on the telephone the night Anna was killed," I continued.

Theda stepped in. "Why would Karl Landrum want to kill that poor woman?" she asked.

"He couldn't resist her temptations," I said. I'd reasoned through the scenario many times in my head. "He kept her in heroin, and she gave back. That escalated, and Shea found out. Or Anna threatened to tell Shea because Anna wanted money to be part of the payment, too."

Theda nodded. She fished a cigarette from her purse. She turned to the street to light it.

"Theda's important in all this," I said. "Anna came to her building the day she died. Theda saw her. Theda's neighbors saw her. She knew her face from the Aguirre séance. So, nothing changes there. Just tell it like you know it."

Theda turned back. "That's exactly how I'll tell it to the police," she said. She blew smoke through her nostrils.

"What do you want us to tell the police?" Addy asked.

Braced by the gin, I asked, "Will you lie for me?"

"Why would we have to do that?" Addy asked.

"To strengthen my case. To undermine Ian's case."

"Of course, we will," Florinda said, glaring at Addy. "What is it that you want us to say?"

"That you visited me in Snowflake. That you were worried about me mingling with the likes of Saint Paul and his cult. That you tried to convince me to leave with you. That I refused. I stayed behind, and you drove back to the city."

Adelaide was quiet. She hesitated.

Theda smiled behind her cigarette like a villain.

"Ian will be so properly miffed about such a thing,"

Florinda said. She watched her sister. "Won't it be delicious to see him squirm?"

"I have one thing to add," Adelaide said finally.

"What's that?" I asked.

"We wouldn't have had to visit you at all if Ian had allowed us to speak to you on the telephone. The moment he left the building, we made the drive out of necessity."

Florinda smiled. "We even left our driver behind since he's under the thumb of Ian. I had to take the wheel. Addy doesn't know how to drive, after all."

"You'd do that for me?" I asked.

"If you only knew how much you've done for the three of us," Addy said, "you wouldn't even think such a thing." She leaned over and hugged me. She embraced me until Thibodeaux grew jealous. He smacked my pant leg with his giant paw.

We went through our plans again, shoring up the details. I wanted everything straight and consistent.

Addy told me more about Ian's past behavior. Once, by prying, he'd ruined an engagement to the man who would've been her second husband.

"I still think we should poison Ian," Florinda said afterwards. "We can recruit his maid to assist us. You know how she feels about him."

"We'll talk about that later," Addy said. She looked at her Pyrenees. "Are you ready for your walk?" she asked. "Are you tired of all this talking? *Se lever*, Thibodeaux. Up, Drucilla."

"They're not reindeer," Florinda said. "Stop that."

"It's cute," Addy said.

I looked at Theda. "Will you go through The Lost Dutchman Mine with me?" I asked.

Coincidence, answered the hagridden man.

The vamp giggled around her cigarette.

"Let's get in line," I said.

CHAPTER TWENTY-FIVE

After dropping off Theda, I made the drive home across town.

Traffic was snarled, and I had little patience for it. I was hot, sweaty, and exhausted from the park. I smacked the wheel a few times out of frustration. I had all four windows down, so everyone near heard my ranting. While we rolled from light to light, I let the news run on the radio. There was nothing on it about Anna Vogel. Nobody cared about a vagrant. If anywhere, she was buried in the back of a newspaper. Once things cooled down, the city would burn her body, and then her ashes would go unclaimed. She'd stay in a canister in a vault until the city cleaned house and sent her to a landfill or dumped her in the sewer where she belonged.

I circled the block until I found a parking spot, and then I pulled to the curb. I wasn't close, so I walked the burning sidewalk with my head down and my hands tucked. It was a nice evening, so there were a lot of pedestrians about. A few kids sat near the mouth of an alley, playing jacks. They didn't bother me, and I didn't bother them. As I neared the entrance to my building, I saw a man sitting on the front stoop. The awning above had him shaded. In that arrangement, he could sit there and wait all day. Maybe he had. He was dressed too uniquely to be mistaken.

The illustrious Saint Paul had decided to grace me with a visit.

My first thought was that the police had summoned him to verify my story. My second thought was that, after some scrutiny, he wanted his money back. Either way the sight had me nervous. I approached like my head was full of daydreams. I greeted Saint Paul with a smile.

He lifted himself from the stone steps. His threads were preposterous. He wore a sleeveless jacket of yellow hemmed with white fur. Beneath this, he was shirtless. His eyes hid behind dark glasses.

"How goes it, my brother?" he said.

We shook hands. He added the flourish of a mudra to that, which I didn't follow.

"You been pannin' for gold, man? Why you so hot?"

I entered the shade and leaned on the rail. "Close enough," I said. "To what do I owe the pleasure, Saint Paul?" I pulled a cigarette and lit it.

"It's Saint Connla now," he said.

"That right?"

He smiled.

"Saint Connla it is."

"I went up and knocked and no one was home, man. Glad I caught you."

Poor Dominic, I thought. *Either he's gone Marilyn Monroe or he's hiding with Ardella under the bed.*

"I'm glad you waited," I said. "I have a favor to ask, but you go first."

"Man, I can't stop thinkin' about the Fairy Maiden story. I want more, brother. I had a dream about it. I wanna do an emergency session. Can you arrange that? I'll pay extra for the trouble. You gotta tease it all out, man."

"When?"

"Like tonight, man." He did a mudra.

"I can arrange that. You have to give me a couple hours, though. How about you meet me back here around eight?"

"You got it, man. Thank you. Now what's your favor, brother?"

I told him to have a seat. He did. I told him about Anna Vogel, and I told him I needed him to corroborate my alibi that I was 150 miles from the crime scene.

"You got it, brother. Fuckin' fascist pigs, man. I don't do cops."

Out of the corner of my eye, I caught the tail end of a green Mercury passing. The car moved slowly, searching for a place to park.

Fuck me, I thought.

Apparently, I was under surveillance. I wondered how long that had been going on. I wondered if that was a line item when Landrum billed Duprey.

Saint Paul/Connla stood to leave. "I'll see you at eight—" he started.

"Hold up," I said. "Why don't you hang around a few more minutes?"

"Why's that, brother? Something wrong?" He looked at the kids playing jacks. "You got gamblin' debts?" He flashed a toothy smile.

I gestured at the sidewalk in the opposite direction. Toward the end of the block, the doors on the Mercury opened.

"You're just in time for Dr. Landrum," I said.

"No shit?" Saint Paul/Connla removed his glasses and looked. "Mrs. Landrum is very fine," he said. "Looks like an old girlfriend." He looked back at me. "You think I could get her to join the ranch, man?"

"Anything's possible," I said. "How many wives do you have?"

He wagged his finger at me.

Landrum's face was already red when he reached the stoop. Shea, as always, was calm, detached. She'd grown tired of her husband's obsession with the chase, I sensed.

"Did eight hours of circling the block finally pay off?" I asked.

"I wasn't surveilling you," Landrum said. "I wanted to speak with you."

"Hey there, Doc," Saint Paul/Connla said. "Mrs. Shea."

"What's he doing here?" Landrum asked. "Are you getting your stories straight? Is that it?"

"Stories about what?" Saint Paul/Connla asked. The face of innocence, he executed a combination of mudras.

Shea frowned, watching his hands.

"A woman was murdered," Karl said. "Mr. Pembrook is under suspicion. He's been traveling around today shoring up his story."

"Yeah, man, I wanted to talk to somebody about that," Saint Paul/Connla said. "That happened to that girl when Doc Madigan was at the ranch, didn't it? That's all the way up in Snowflake."

I nodded.

"It occurred at that time, yes," Landrum said.

"Yeah, brother, I need a pig to jot it down. Doc Madigan was by my side all night. I didn't let him outta my sight. Hell, man, I was payin' him. Brother had a leash on. I ain't frivolous with money, man. I ain't a fool."

Outwardly, I stayed neutral. Inwardly, I thought, *you're*

not going to pay at all for tonight's session, Connla. This one's on me. I patted my friend on the shoulder.

"That's right," I said. "He's a tough taskmaster."

Karl closed his eyes in frustration. He saw the hill before him turn into a mountain. Futility surfaced in his eyes.

"What's wrong?" I asked. "Is your alibi not so tight as that?" I looked at Shea. "You realize what your old man was doing with Anna, don't you? You realize all she was doing in return for the heroin?"

"You're sick," Shea said.

Saint Paul/Connla stood and returned the slap on the shoulder. "Find me a pig to talk to, brother," he said. "I'll set him straight. I'll see you tonight." He started away down the sidewalk.

I shrugged at Karl. "I don't think he likes the APRO," I said. "He's got a thing about skeptics."

Shea, flummoxed, went back to the Mercury. I figured Karl would get some of the heat building in her head. By the way he watched her, he figured the same.

I stepped down to the sidewalk, eye to eye with Landrum.

"I'm going to tell you two things," I said. "First, I'm going to bust open your skull if I ever get the chance."

His mouth tightened. "Is that right?" he said. "You did kill her, didn't you?"

"Second, I'm going to bury you in Ian Duprey's backyard."

"You're fucking scum," Landrum said.

I shrugged. I flicked ashes onto his alligator shoes.

"You're a con, Pembrook. You're nothing but a lowlife, piece of shit."

"That's true," I said. I blew smoke from the corner of my mouth. "And there's nothing you or Ian Duprey can do about it."

Karl's blood pressure tipped the needle. He was red all the way up his neck and face.

"There's a third thing," I said. I crushed the cigarette against concrete. "It probably won't make you happy, Karl, but I saw three beige Cadillac Sedans in traffic today." I looked down the street at a red light. "There's a fourth."

He turned to see.

"Unfortunately, it's a popular model," I said.

CHAPTER TWENTY-SIX

There are several points in the Superstition Mountains that command breathtaking vistas. It's gorgeous country. It isn't difficult to imagine how gold-mine legends gestate in such surroundings. Dom and I were hiking a path called the Hieroglyphic Trail. It was one of the easy trails with a lot of rocks, prickly pear, some incline, and points of shade through the morning. If you hit the trail at the right time of year, the hike culminates with a waterfall surrounded by ancient Indian petroglyphs. Saint Paul/Connla had recommended it.

Looking back at the descending valley behind us, I stopped. I pointed out flat ground shaded by a rock face.

"Here should work," I said.

Dominic gripped his backpack. He was having a blast. He seemed happy.

We unfurled a blanket on the ground. From my pack, I pulled out the same transistor radio that Dom and I had listened to during our first date, thirteen years prior. I'd taken the radio to a repair shop, had it fixed. It was up and running, tinny and staticky as ever.

Dom smiled when he saw it.

"You fixed it?" he said.

"Sure did."

I switched it on and scrolled through the AM dial. Few stations reached this desolate valley, but I found one that played classics. It came through with a hiss. The song was "Sh-Boom" by The Chords.

"Now that's music," I said.

"You're a dinosaur," Dom said.

I smiled. "Yeah. Kids these days don't know good music."

He laughed. He reached over and rubbed my neck.

The waterfall cascaded up ahead, and the sound spreading down the valley was peaceful.

"Thank you for coming out here," Dom said. "I know this isn't who you are."

"I haven't complained once," I said. "As promised."

Dom stretched his legs and put his arms behind him to balance. He watched the sky.

"I read something interesting in the paper this morning," I said.

"Go ahead."

"Ian Duprey died last night."

His smiled faded. He turned from the sky to me. "You're kidding. The brother?"

"Cardiac arrest," I said. "Peaceful, I suppose. Died in his sleep."

"Did you telephone Addy and Florinda?"

I shook my head. "I planned on driving over there tonight. You can't simply telephone about a tragedy like that."

"You should've called, Royce. It's gentlemanly."

"I didn't want to interrupt the celebration. By now, wine's flowing like the Tiber."

"You're not funny. A heart attack is so sudden. I imagine they're shell-shocked."

"There are at least two people who saw it coming," I said. "Perhaps three if you include the maid."

"What are you talking about?"

"I'm only kidding. It's tragic."

Dominic frowned at me. He sat up and lit a clove cigarette. I took out a cigarette, too.

"I see you're back to kings," Dom said.

"Health," I said. "Getting old means temperance."

"You're not cutting off the filters, are you?"

"Nope." I smoked a little and remembered. "You know what else I read in the paper?"

Dom didn't say anything.

"Remember that jackass who brought the London Bridge to Lake Havasu? He's going to rededicate it in a couple years. How tacky is that?"

Dom laughed. "I still want to visit," he said.

"I figured." Looking at one of the distant cliffs, I asked, "Do you remember when we watched *Lust for Gold* on the sofa together? It's about the Lost Dutchman's Mine. It has Glenn Ford and Ida Lupino. Ardella was stretched out on the back of the couch. We were in the living room in the dark, cuddled up."

"How many times are you going to ask me that?" Dom said. "No, Royce, I don't. That didn't happen. I've never seen it."

"Do you remember how we mocked the guy screaming as he fell over the cliff? We laughed about that shriek for weeks," I said.

Dominic fell silent. He watched me. "How many times are you going to ask about that movie?" he repeated.

Until you say yes, I thought, watching the cliff.

I reached over and turned up the radio. Doo-wop sounded good over the rocks, blending with the cascading water above.

"I told Anna Vogel about it," I said. I waved my hand over the vista that stretched below. "Somewhere out there, somewhere by the road, I told Anna all about that night, Dom. I told her we were happy."

ACKNOWLEDGMENTS

———

My gratitude and thanks to the following authors for their guidance, support, and friendship:

Michael August	Remo Macartney
Garth Arizona	Catherine McCarthy
Brian Berry	Ronald McGillvray
C.W. Blackwell	Joe Nelson
Brian Bowyer	Tim McGregor
Stephanie Ellis	Jennifer Ostopovich
Adam Hulse	Anthony Perconti
Derek Hutchins	Ron Earl Phillips
Sean Jacques	M.E. Proctor
Russell W. Johnson	Mark Robinson
Zakariah Johnson	Michael Shotter
DS LaLonde	Jonathan Tripp
Meagan Lucas	Ilyn Welch
Regan MacArthur	

Coy Hall lives in West Virginia, where he splits time as an author and professor of history. His books include *Grimoire of the Four Impostors* (2021), *The Hangman Feeds the Jackal: A Gothic Western* (2022), and *The Promise of Plague Wolves* (2023). Find him at www.coyhall.com.

ABOUT
SHOTGUN HONEY
BOOKS

Thank you for reading *The Switchblade Svengali* by Coy Hall.

Shotgun Honey began as a crime genre flash fiction webzine in 2011 created as a venue for new and established writers to experiment in the confines of a mere 700 words. More than a decade later, Shotgun Honey still challenges writers with that storytelling task, but also provides opportunities to expand beyond through our book imprint and has since published anthologies, collections, novellas and novels by new and emerging authors.

We hope you have enjoyed this book. That you will share your experience, review and rate this title positively on your favorite book review sites and with your social media family and friends.

Visit ShotgunHoneyBooks.com

SHOTGUN HONEY
FICTION WITH A KICK